BREAKING NEWS

•

Janet Boling

AVALON BOOKS
NEW YORK

Published by Thomas Bouregy & Co., Inc.
160 Madison Avenue, New York, NY 10016

Library of Congress Cataloging-in-Publication Data

Boling, Janet.
    Breaking news / Janet Boling.
        p. cm.
    ISBN 978-0-8034-9848-8 (acid-free paper) 1. Women news-
paper editors—Fiction. 2. Michigan—Fiction. I. Title.

    PS3602.O654B74 2007
    813'.6—dc22

                                        2007011969

PRINTED IN THE UNITED STATES OF AMERICA
ON ACID-FREE PAPER
BY HADDON CRAFTSMEN, BLOOMSBURG, PENNSYLVANIA

For Molly and Patrick,
who have the proudest mother on earth.

Prologue

The professor sighed, branded a red F on the exam, and shoved the paper to the side of his desk. It sealed this student's fate. He'd probably flunk Ancient History.

He leaned back in his chair and folded his arms. Professor Lichner hated failing a student. And it happened all too often. Hardly anyone did well in his class. *Is it my fault?* he asked himself with fleeting thoughts of a career change—tempting because of everything else that was going on . . .

He looked out the classroom windows. It was dark, already evening. What was it he always heard people say about teachers? Something about short workdays and summers off? He chuckled out loud.

His gaze drifted to the reflection of the classroom door in the windows, where a lone figure stood. Turning his head, Lichner recognized the visitor.

1

"You're kind of late. My decision has been made and it's final," he said, not wanting to talk about the problem now. It had been a long day and he still had one more commitment before going home.

"I know. I'm not here to discuss it with you."

Lichner shrugged his shoulders and stood, grabbing an eraser off the chalkboard ledge.

"This could have been avoided, you know," he said, turning away from his visitor as his weary strokes brushed the essay questions about the Roman empire off the board. "The choices you made, they just—"

The visitor pulled a knife from a deep raincoat pocket and ended the conversation with a thrust at the professor's back.

Putting the bloodied weapon back in the pocket, the murderer stepped into the empty hallway and slipped out the building door, into the evening darkness.

Chapter One

Sarah Carpenter tossed the bridal magazine she was reading onto the coffee table. If she wanted to be on time for her interview with the history professor she'd have to haul herself off her cozy couch and head out the door of her Lake Michigan cottage.

She hadn't been thrilled when the professor told her the interview would need to be scheduled in the evening. Her nights were full enough as it was, covering various municipal and school board meetings for the *Potter County Times* newspaper. When she left her reporting job at a Chicago daily newspaper to become editor of the *Times*, she never expected such long hours. But being able to move to her dream lake cottage in the northwest corner of Michigan's Lower Peninsula made up for the headaches inherent in running a small, short-staffed newspaper. And the bonus of meeting the man she was going to marry helped lighten the load too.

Sarah stood, tucking her tailored white shirt more neatly into the jeans she'd put on after work. Hoping the professor didn't mind her casual appearance but too tired to change, she grabbed a tan cotton blazer from her bedroom closet to dress up her outfit a bit. She dropped a pen in its breast pocket and hurriedly ran a brush through her shoulder-length, chestnut-brown hair.

The pine-plank flooring of her tiny home creaked as she headed to the kitchen for the keys to her pickup truck. She adored this house, nestled among beach grasses just a few hundred feet from the shoreline. From the clapboard siding to the temperamental septic system, it had been the recipient of continuous rehabilitation. Never before, though, had she grown so attached to a dwelling.

Stepping out her door and onto her porch, she heard forceful waves powered by a strong, springtime wind breaking on the Lake Michigan shore. The warmer months were always a busy time at the newspaper in this resort area. Advertisers required more space, so the news side had to hold its own too. Sarah often found herself assigning reporters to cover the local craft shows, flower sales and pie-eating contests—anything to fill a hole on the news pages.

She turned her key in the brass doorknob, smiling as always when she heard the lock mechanism's reassuring click. She used to leave her place unlocked. It had made no difference because her old door and lock were so feeble that a determined intruder could gain entry with the slightest push of a hand. But her fiancé, aware that Sarah's job sometimes put her in contact with unsavory characters, promptly purchased safer doors for her little house when the doorknob once came loose in his hand.

She headed the pickup down her long gravel driveway and toward Hillcrest, the town fifteen minutes away where both the *Times* and the community college were located. Sarah needed to interview Professor Philip Lichner for a feature story she was preparing on the town of Hillcrest's one-hundred-and-fiftieth anniversary of incorporation. As president of the Hillcrest Historical Society, the professor was the area's best source for background.

As the highway curved away from Lake Michigan and toward the inland lakes and forests surrounding Hillcrest, Sarah cracked the window of the pickup. She inhaled the sweet aroma of damp woods and wild trillium blossoms. Soon the area would be swarming with summer residents and visitors but she didn't mind. They had fallen in love with this beautiful place, just like she had.

The two-year, tax-supported community college was located on prime land fronting Sapphire Lake, named for its brilliant blue color. Local developers for years had drooled at the thought of purchasing the property and building exclusive multi-family dwellings, a big moneymaker in residential projects. Despite a downturn in college enrollment, the school's board of trustees consistently rejected proposals to sell the land and move its operation to more cost-efficient space. In fact, the board was enmeshed in a controversial rehabilitation of the campus' six one-hundred-year-old buildings.

Sarah pulled her pickup into the parking lot near the administration building. It and the social sciences building, where she was to meet the professor, were the only modern structures on campus. Most classrooms and teachers' offices were housed in stately, turreted buildings constructed in red brick with terra cotta ornamentation.

She looked at the time on her dashboard. Needing to kill another ten minutes before her interview, she stopped in the administration building, where a boisterous public meeting was underway. She knew that the *Times'* only full-time reporter, Holly James, was there covering it.

She peeked into the meeting room.

"When you proposed this project, you promised us better facilities, and what do we get?" a red-faced woman was shouting. "Half-finished projects at a huge cost! What are you going to do about it? We're the ones who are footing the bill, and we want some answers!"

The board president, Beth Callison, raised her hand to quiet the chorus of jeers in the packed room.

"You must realize that renovating historic buildings is a huge undertaking, and all that money did not come from the building fund. You have to realize that . . ."

A man stood and pointed a finger at her before she could finish. "We realize that you've taken money from the taxpayers and thrown it away! Your whole board fooled us, and you're not going to get away with it! Where are the other administrators? Why aren't they here?"

Sarah noticed a campus security guard in the room and realized the board was wise to have him there. A roomful of angry taxpayers was unpredictable, and this group had turned surly. She saw Holly sitting in the front row with her notebook poised on her lap and pen racing across it. Holly looked up at Sarah, checked her watch and rolled her eyes. She knew it would be a long night.

The editor grinned at her tired reporter and gave a small wave, heading out the door toward the social sciences building. Professor Lichner had told her to meet him at eight o'clock. He had a late afternoon class, he had said, and wanted to finish grading some papers before the interview.

The camera she had slung over her shoulder bounced on her hip as she crossed the concrete courtyard separating the two buildings. The professor said he had an old map of the area hanging on his classroom wall. She'd take a photo of him with it, pointing to Hillcrest's location. Not an exciting shot, but a much-needed space filler.

She nodded hello to a janitor who had just stepped off the elevator, hauling a floor polisher behind him.

"I think all the classes are over for tonight, ma'am," he said. "Is there something I can help you with?"

She shook her head. "No, thanks. I have an appointment with a professor just down the hall here. Thank you anyway."

The janitor smiled, hiked up his drooping trousers and started whistling, dragging the machine away from her as his tune echoed in the hallway.

She passed darkened, empty classrooms as she made her way to Room 126, where Professor Lichner told her he'd be waiting. Looking out the glass-walled hallway windows on her left, she noticed drops of rain hitting the panes and flowering courtyard redbud trees bending in a strengthening wind. She hoped the rain would last all night. The sounds of a storm and crashing Lake Michigan waves always lulled her to sleep after a busy day.

Light from Room 126 spilled onto the hallway floor, signaling to her that she'd found it. She stepped in, saw an empty teacher's desk, and scanned the room for the professor. He wasn't there.

Checking her watch, she saw that it was precisely eight o'clock. It appeared that the professor had left some papers on the desk. Maybe he stepped out to get a cup of coffee from a vending machine, she thought. Or maybe he had to run over to his office to get information for the interview.

"Hmm. Guess I'll just have to wait," she mumbled aloud.

She lifted the camera off her shoulder and set it and her notebook on a desk in the front row. Deciding to wait about ten minutes before trying to find him elsewhere, she slid into the student desk and put her chin in her hand, looking at the floor.

That's when she saw him.

The crumpled body of a man was wedged between the corner of the teacher's desk and the blackboard wall. Hidden from a doorway view, the body was twisted and its head was awkwardly bent against the baseboard.

Sarah bolted from the desk, her leg catching the top of it and sending her camera crashing to the floor.

"Oh, my God. Professor? Professor Lichner?"

She approached him quickly, then jumped back from a pool of blood surrounding the man's upper torso. His shirt was soaked with a crimson stain.

"Oh, no . . . please, no." She avoided the gruesome puddle as she kneeled next to the body. Despite her shock, she knew she had to do something. She had to see if he might still be alive.

What had she been taught in a CPR class many years ago? Check his pulse and see if he's breathing, she remembered. Start the technique if there's any sign of life—but how can she do that as well as call for help?

"Help! Anybody! Help! In Room One-twenty-six!" she shouted. Then, lifting a shaking hand, she leaned over the body and held her fingers to the man's neck, hoping to feel a pulse.

She couldn't detect even the tiniest motion of life. And his open but unseeing, glassy eyes stared ahead with a vacancy that confirmed for her that this man, probably Professor Lichner, was dead.

Rubbing her hands on her jeans as she stood, subconsciously wiping off the feel of death, she backed away from the body. No one had responded to her frantic calls. She had left her cell phone in the pickup, so she knew she had to leave the body and seek help somewhere else.

Sarah stepped into the hallway, once again shouting for help. Waiting a minute, she called out again. No one came.

Where's that janitor? She was uneasy at the thought of leaving what looked like an obvious crime scene. It was against a reporter's nature to walk away from a probable murder story while it was still unfolding, but she knew she had to get an ambulance and the police there immediately.

The security guard! She hurried down the hallway and then broke into a jog as she left the building and headed for the board of trustees meeting in the administration building.

She was relieved to see the guard standing at the meeting room doorway, where she could discreetly tell him what had happened and not interrupt the proceedings. That surely would have attracted a crowd to Room One-two-six, making it more difficult for authorities to handle it and for her to report on it.

She lightly touched his arm, getting his attention.

"Excuse me," she whispered, out-of-breath and agitated. "I think it's Professor Lichner . . . in Room One-twenty-six in the social sciences building. You need to go there . . . I think he's dead . . . maybe murdered."

"What?" His eyes widened and his hand instinctively covered his holstered gun at the report of danger. "Show me."

They rushed to the other building as Sarah tried to calm herself and describe what she had seen. She explained who she was, why she was there, and what she had found. The security guard, not sure what he was about to face, silently took in all the information as they approached the room.

A floor polisher was outside the door, and the guard gave Sarah a puzzled look.

"It's the janitor," she said. "He must have heard me shouting."

They entered the room, where the stunned maintenance man stood staring at the body. Tearing his gaze away from the lifeless form when he heard them arrive, he slowly lifted his arm and pointed at the dead figure, his mouth agape.

"It's Professor Lichner," he breathed. "He's . . . dead."

"I was calling for you when I found him," Sarah told him as the guard took in the scene. "Did you hear me?"

The janitor nodded, his face suddenly growing pale as he sank into a student desk.

The guard, who was kneeling beside the body, pulled his portable radio from its jacket and ordered a dispatcher to send an ambulance and report the death to the sheriff's department. Noticeably rattled, he turned to the janitor and Sarah.

"You two have to leave. You can't be hanging around here. This is a crime scene. I have to secure it and I can't do that with you in the way."

Sarah shook her head. "I believe the police will want me here when they arrive so I can tell them what happened. And as a reporter, I have a right to be here, at least until I talk to the police myself."

The security guard had never dealt with reporters before and didn't much like her being around. But he knew she was correct—she was a witness—and he didn't want to get into any hassle with the newspaper. He figured he'd let the cops handle it.

"Well, all right," he relented. "But do me a favor and wait in the hallway. I don't want anyone disturbing the scene before the county guys get here."

Sarah decided that was good enough and bent to retrieve her camera on the floor. Although her news judgment immediately declared the image of Professor Lichner's body as too gruesome to print in the *Times,* some shots of the room with soon-to-arrive investigators would be appropriate.

"I said, I don't want anyone to disturb the scene!" the guard barked, his patience waning as the gravity of the situation sank in. "Leave the camera alone and get out of here!"

Her years in the newspaper business had left Sarah with little patience for law-enforcement types who treated reporters like criminal trespassers, ordering them around as if the rights of a free press didn't exist. And this guy wasn't even a genuine police officer.

"Hey, calm down, buddy!" she shot back. "I dropped that when I saw the body and it has nothing to do with the crime. But if you're going to be so uptight about it, I'll leave it there until the cops show up, okay?"

Steamed, she exhaled loudly and followed the janitor into the hall, deftly grabbing her notebook off the student desk without being seen. The janitor was ending a call to his wife on a cell phone, his words nervously stuttered as he let her know he'd be home late and why.

Sarah folded her arms and leaned against the wall, hearing the sound of approaching sirens. Once the sheriff's deputies showed up, she'd probably have little chance of prying any information from them. They resented reporters more than the security guard.

She lightly tapped her foot on the hallway's tile floor, thinking. She wanted to stick around as long as possible, maybe take a few photos and get the best story she could before tomorrow's deadline. If she wanted to have any chance of an extended stay at the scene of this murder, though, she'd need some help from the powers-that-be.

Sarah asked the janitor if she could borrow his phone, hoping she'd be able to reach her best source on the Potter County Sheriff's Department. If her source told the deputies to let her stay on the scene, she was sure they wouldn't dare toss her out.

They had to listen to Sheriff Mark Browning—her fiancé.

Chapter Two

"I should have guessed you'd get there before me. Tell me you're planning to leave. Please."

An exasperated Mark Browning closed his eyes and kneaded his forehead as he listened to his fiancée plead her case for staying on the scene of a murder. He was trying to massage away a sprouting headache.

"No, I'm not planning to leave and I know they're going to try to kick me out of here," Sarah was telling him. "They can't do that, Mark. I'm the one who found the body. Shouldn't you tell your investigators to keep me here so they can interview me?"

Browning's eyes popped open. "You found the body? How . . . what . . . how did that happen? What were you doing over at the college?"

"My interview for Hillcrest's one-hundred-and-fiftieth anniversary, remember? I had an appointment with Professor Lichner. He knows . . . knew . . . all about the town's history."

Browning sighed. Sarah's phone call had interrupted his exit from his apartment after receiving a phone call from the sheriff's department radio room about a suspicious death at the community college. He guessed he'd run into his news-hungry fiancée over there and that was distracting enough to an investigation. But finding out she was a critical witness just complicated matters even more.

"Okay, listen," Browning began. "Just stay out of the way over there, don't ask any questions and don't snoop around the scene. I know—"

"I think I have a right to ask questions, Mark. After all, I'm—"

"Sarah, you know how I feel about reporters interfering with our work, and I'd rather you not cause a commotion before I even get there. Unfortunately, you have to stay there for now because we need to talk to you. I'll get in touch with my guys and let them know that, but please be cooperative and don't act like . . . a reporter."

Sarah feigned hurt feelings. "Hey, is that any way to talk to the woman you love? I mean, to the *reporter* you love?"

Browning grinned, bracing the phone between ear and shoulder as he strapped his gun and holster onto his jeans belt. "You deserve it. You might be an incredibly wonderful woman, but you're also the most pesky reporter I've ever met."

Sarah smiled too. "Why, thank you, Sheriff. See you soon."

Browning hung up and dialed his detective's car phone number, confirming that medical examiner Sam "Doc" Fellows and evidence technician Joe Barone had been called to the scene. Then he apologetically told him that it was a reporter who found the body and warned him that questioning this person might be a little more difficult than most, usually perfunctory, witness interviews.

"And, uh, by the way, Charlie," he told his investigator. "The reporter is Sarah."

Detective Thompson chuckled. "So you're telling me that when I say, 'Thanks for your time, ma'am. You can leave now,' she ain't gonna leave, right?"

Browning grabbed his keys off the kitchen table. "You know Sarah, Charlie. She'll be hounding us for all the details. The worst part is that she probably knows more than us right now. Nothing is more dangerous than a reporter with too much information."

Thompson whistled through his teeth. "Never a dull moment with you two, huh? I'm sure the guys at the scene will get a kick out of seeing their sheriff having a lovers' spat with the editor of the local newspaper!"

Browning laughed and said good-bye. Thompson was able to get away with teasing his boss, having closely worked with him on several cases after Browning left his job as a New York City detective to fill the Potter County undersheriff position, later winning the sheriff's job in a bitter election.

Browning trotted down the stairs from his apartment, a sparsely furnished but functional space above an art store in downtown Hillcrest. He had rented it as a temporary residence when he moved to Michigan, hoping to find a home on one of the inland lakes that had lured him to the area in the first place. His quick attraction and eventual engagement to Sarah, though, put a hold on his plans. Her cottage on Lake Michigan was gorgeous and just big enough for two—they'd make their home there after the wedding.

As he drove toward the college, he drummed his fingers on the steering wheel of his unmarked Chevy. The politicians would definitely be questioning him about this murder, worried that city-like crime problems had reached their resort area. They'd remind him that it wasn't good for business. He was expecting some hard questions from the newspaper too. He was sure Sarah would cover the front page with this story until he solved it.

The timing of this crime couldn't have been worse, he told himself. Any time he was working on a big case, their relationship was tested. Sarah's job required her to dig for news, question the authorities and present as much information as possible to the public. But his job was to solve crimes, protect pertinent facts in order to build a solid case, and keep nosy reporters at bay. While their love for each other always managed to overcome career conflicts, it could be a strain.

And the wedding was only three months away.

A few people watching the school board deliberate heard the wail of sirens above the heated words being exchanged in the meeting room, and their curiosity led them to the social sciences building. A deputy posted outside blocked their entrance as they strained to peer inside the windows, hoping to see what brought the flood of emergency vehicles to the normally crime-free campus.

Browning grabbed his portable radio off the passenger seat, surveyed the nosy group that continued to accumulate outside the building and swung his long legs out of the car. Wind and rain whipped through his nearly black hair, which he combed off his forehead with his fingers as he headed to the crime scene. The deputy nodded hello to Browning and opened the school building door for his boss, turning away a young woman in the crowd who tried to slip inside behind the sheriff.

The first person he spotted was Sarah, sullenly leaning against the polished, stone-block hallway wall, notebook in hand. The janitor was seated cross-legged on the floor, his head resting against the opposite wall. Sarah turned at the sound of Browning's approach and stepped away from the wall. Her heart always soared when she saw the man she loved, but she needed to look businesslike now. She folded her arms and sported an annoyed expression. He knew what was coming.

"Mark," she began, softening her look because she knew aggression would get her nowhere with him, "they haven't even tried to talk to me yet. I'm their best source of information so far, but Thompson told me to wait out here until he's ready to question me. The person who did this could be miles away by now. Do you guys always operate this way?"

Browning rubbed his chin, forcing back the urge to kiss her hello. Watching her fierce devotion to her job from the time they first met made him love her even more, as frustrating as it often could be.

"I see. And I suppose you want to speak to my detective as soon as possible only because of your concern in wanting to help us catch this person quickly. I'm sure it has nothing to do with the fact that you need information for a quickly approaching deadline."

Sarah tried her best to maintain a deadpan look. "That never entered my mind. I'm just surprised you'd leave a crucial witness standing out here so long."

Thompson had heard the sheriff's voice and poked his head out the door, motioning for him to come inside the classroom.

"Sarah," Browning said as he acknowledged Thompson, "you found the body. As I understand it, you didn't see anyone or anything else that would help us. We'll talk with you more after we take care of some other business first. Just wait here and . . . please . . .

don't try to come into the room or listen at the door or whatever it is that you reporters do."

Sarah rolled her green eyes and slumped back against the wall, glancing at the janitor who had been listening intently to the conversation.

"You two know each other?" he asked with a curious lift of his eyebrows.

A small smile played on her lips. "We see each other from time to time through our jobs," she told him, dryly adding, "plus, we're getting married in three months."

The janitor pointed at her. "Oh, yeah, I heard about you two. You're the editor who's going to marry our sheriff, huh? Wasn't there some big stink about that during the election? What was with all that anyway?"

Sarah waved off the question. "Oh, just some political stuff. Mark's opponent tried to make people believe that I was making him look good in the newspaper so that he'd win the election. But, as you can tell from the conversation you just heard, I treat him like everyone else."

The janitor nodded. "Yeah, I can see that. Should be an interesting marriage."

Sarah didn't know exactly how he meant that and ended the conversation with a quick smile. She edged nearer to the door and sat on the floor, laying down her notebook and resting her head against the wall. One ear was cocked for sounds from within the room.

* * *

Browning was crouching over the body, visually examining every detail of the lifeless form in search of any clues the killer had left behind. He studied the blood-soaked shirt, noted an eraser lying near the body, then glanced up at the blackboard.

"No blood splatters on the wall," Thompson told him. "I doubt that a gun was the weapon. Looks like he took a knife to the back, or something else just as sharp."

Browning raised an eyebrow. "Our offender must have had pretty good aim. Looks like the good professor here went down pretty quick. Stabbing victims usually aren't disabled so quickly, but it appears he didn't have a chance to move from this spot."

Thompson agreed. "There's no blood anywhere else to indicate there was any kind of struggle. He must've never seen it coming and was hurt too bad to move afterwards. That eraser on the floor tells me he was cleaning the board."

Browning's eyes scanned the room. "You got our guys searching inside and outside the building for a possible weapon yet?"

The detective nodded as his fingers searched for his belt, hidden beneath a generous belly that displayed his love of good food. He hiked up his trousers and reached in his pocket for a stick of gum.

"Yeah, and Barone and Doc Fellows should be here shortly. The security guard managed to keep the scene clean until we arrived. I hear he even kicked your fiancée out of here," Thompson said with a sly smile.

"I've had to do that a couple of times myself, Charlie." Browning stepped back from the blackboard to take a look at the half-erased words. "What's this say? 'Explain the economic conditions during the Fall of . . .' What did this guy teach, do you know, Charlie?"

Thompson moved the wad of gum to the side of his mouth and ran his fingertips through his dwindling strands of hair. "Some kind of history. That's what the security guard says. He isn't sure, but he knows most of the rooms in this area are for history classes."

Browning rubbed his chin. "It looks like he had questions written on the board, maybe for a test. That's probably what these papers are on his desk. We need to check on his schedule and talk to his students," he told Thompson as his detective jotted notes in a small memo pad.

They heard familiar voices in the hall as Doc Fellows and Barone greeted Sarah, who continued to wait outside the room with increasing curiosity. She tried to ease inside the door behind the law enforcement pros, but Browning caught her in the act.

"Sarah! Wait outside!" Then, more gently, he added, "We'll be with you in a little bit, all right?"

She looked at her watch and folded her arms into an impatient stance, reminding him with her body language that she was a reporter on deadline in need of information. And she knew that was the least of his concerns at the moment.

"What've we got here, Mark?" Doc Fellows asked, pulling his wire-rimmed glasses down off their perch on his white hair. He bent his tall, thin frame over the professor's body.

"Looks like a stabbing, Doc. We don't have the weapon, so we'll need your help in figuring that one out. Whatever was used, we're guessing it did its job pretty quickly."

Doc's knees made cracking sounds as he slowly straightened up, massaging his seventy-year-old back and moving away from the body so Barone could video-tape the scene. He waited for the evidence technician to film the professor from all angles before crouching down again to make his official pronouncement of death.

"I'll be getting to work on him as soon as you boys deliver him to my office," Doc said. "I'll get my autopsy report to you ASAP, Mark."

Barone finished videotaping and began unloading materials from his evidence collection case, humming softly as he began his task. The evidence technician, short and stocky with a precisely trimmed crew cut, loved his work.

"Charlie and I got a couple witnesses we need to interview in the hall, Joe," Browning told him. "Let us know if you have any questions."

Barone nodded as he began to collect hair and fiber evidence near the body with a portable vacuum, which would be packaged and delivered to the crime lab along with other items he deemed important.

"You already interviewed the security guard, right Charlie?" Browning asked his detective as they stepped into the hall. "How about you talk to Sarah and I'll take the janitor?"

Thompson chuckled. "Yeah, I think that would be the wise thing to do. You going to be part of the investigation? Are you sure you got the time?"

Browning shrugged. "I'm going to have to make time, Charlie. You know how uneasy our local politicians get when there's a major crime in our fair county. They're going to have questions, and I better have the answers."

Sarah wasn't getting the information she needed from Thompson.

"I'm interviewing you as a witness, Ms. Carpenter," Thompson kept telling her. "I'm not here to be interviewed by you. You can ask the sheriff your newspaper questions when he has the time."

She glanced over at Mark, who was still talking to the janitor. "He's still busy, Detective. All I need to know is the manner of death and whether there's been any information leading to a suspect. Was he shot? Do you think a student might be responsible?"

Thompson ignored her questions and continued with his own. "So, you arrived here for an appointment with the professor, you found him on the floor and immediately sought help, right?" he said, reading his notebook. "You didn't see anyone else here before or after you arrived?"

Sarah sighed. "Like I told you three times, the only

person I saw was the janitor, who was getting off the elevator when I arrived. I didn't see anyone when I left, but the janitor was here when the security guard and I returned to the room. Do you consider the janitor to be a suspect?"

The detective focused narrowed eyes on her, indicating that he was becoming increasingly displeased with her search for information. "Did the professor sound nervous or upset when you made the appointment to see him tonight?" he asked in a slightly annoyed tone.

She slowly shook her head. "No, although he wasn't as talkative as another time I called him for information about Hillcrest history. He was kind of short with me, like this appointment was a bother for him and he wouldn't have much time."

Thompson stopped scribbling and lifted interested eyes beneath heavy lids. "Did he say whether he had other business to take care of tonight?"

She tapped her lip with an index finger and squeezed her eyes shut, searching her memory. "Oh, yes! He said he'd be grading papers before our appointment because he was giving an essay exam today. That's why he couldn't meet with me right after his five o'clock class."

She looked over Thompson's shoulder and saw the janitor walking down the hallway with a deputy. Mark was paging through his notes and walking back into the classroom.

"Mark! Wait a second!" she called out, starting out toward him.

"Hey, *you* wait a second, Ms. Carpenter,"

Thompson growled. "Who says I'm finished with you yet?"

Sarah put her hands on her hips. "Are you?"

Thompson hesitated. "Well, yeah, but I'm sure the sheriff will tell you exactly what I'm telling you—we don't have any information for you media people yet."

She flashed a confident smile. "Check out the front page story in Wednesday's issue and see if you're right, Detective."

Browning walked over to her as she retrieved her notebook from the hallway floor. He jammed his memo pad into the back pocket of his jeans and folded his arms, waiting for her onslaught of questions and ready with responses.

"So," Sarah began as she lifted her pen from her blazer's breast pocket, struggling to maintain a professional tone as he focused his gorgeous eyes on her. "How was he killed and are there any suspects?"

Browning scratched his cheek and sighed. "Sarah, the body hasn't even left the room yet. Doc has to examine him to determine the cause of death, and I'm not saying a word about any suspects, got it? All I can tell you is that Professor Philip Lichner is dead and the Potter County Sheriff's Department is investigating."

She had expected the stonewalling and it didn't faze her. "Can anyone you interviewed be considered a suspect?" she pressed, thinking about the janitor.

Browning stepped closer to her and cupped his hand over his mouth. "Well," he whispered, "this is off the record, but we did talk to a one Sarah Carpenter of the *Potter County Times* who seemed awfully suspicious."

Sarah pursed her lips and narrowed her eyes. "Not funny, Mark. You want me to start making jokes about *your* job?"

He put his hand on her shoulder, squeezing it gently. "I'm sorry. I know you have to ask these questions, but I really have nothing to tell you right now. I'll have the cause of death for you by tomorrow morning. Other than that, you know we can't get into any other information we're investigating."

She dropped her pen back into her pocket and tossed her hair away from her face. She'd have to wait until the next day to write the story anyway, she thought, so the latest news would be available.

"I suppose I won't see you tonight, huh? Should I call you at the office tomorrow morning? My deadline is ten o'clock."

He remembered that he was going to stop by her house a little later and take her to the new ice cream parlor that had opened in Hillcrest. They'd both been so busy lately that it would have been their first night out together in more than a week.

"I'll be tied up all night with this," he sighed, wishing he could cover her lips with his to remind her how much he'd been missing their quiet moments together. "I'll sure be wanting to hear your voice first before I go to bed tonight, so . . ."

They were interrupted by a deputy accompanied by

a young woman with short blond hair and a shapely figure that Sarah was sure Mark would notice. She guessed her age to be about twenty, and the deputy wasn't much older.

"Excuse me, Sheriff, but this . . . er . . . lady here says she has some information that might be helpful. Her name is Heather Bergen and she says the professor had been having some trouble lately with one of his students."

Browning winced and Sarah snapped her notebook open again, reaching for her pen.

The deputy paled as he watched Sarah record his remarks. "Gee . . . um . . . I'm sorry, sir. I didn't realize she's a reporter or something."

Browning rubbed his forehead, the brief silence making it clear to the deputy that he'd just screwed up. "Sarah, call me in the morning. Deputy, please make sure Ms. Carpenter is kept away from the scene and I'll talk to the young lady here. But I need to speak with you for a moment when I'm finished."

The chagrined deputy nodded and Sarah winked at Mark, smiling broadly as she turned to leave.

She knew what the topic of their morning conversation would be.

Chapter Three

After taking the deputy aside and explaining to him the advantages of keeping his mouth shut during a murder investigation, Browning returned to the young woman waiting in the hall. She was biting a lip slathered in pink frost lipstick and twirling a short strand of platinum hair with her finger.

Browning had recognized her immediately. In a criminal justice class he taught at the college the previous semester, she'd been an enthusiastic student with endless questions who often paused after class to discuss law enforcement issues with him. She had become almost an annoyance, as he wasn't sure if she was fascinated with legal issues or with him.

"Sorry to keep you waiting, Miss . . ." He hesitated, forgetting her name.

"Bergen. Heather Bergen. Remember? I was in your class last semester."

Browning nodded. "Yes, I know. I'm sorry—it's been a while. I remember that you did very well in my class."

Heather smiled broadly, displaying perfect, white teeth. "I absolutely loved your class! You're a great teacher, Sheriff. I was so disappointed that you didn't have a class this semester."

"I like teaching once in a while, but the job keeps me pretty busy. So, I understand you have information about the professor. Tell me, how did you learn about his death?"

Heather shrugged. "I guess I just overheard people outside talking about it. I walked over here from the library when I saw the crowd. Everyone's gabbing about it out there."

Browning expected word to spread. It could have started with the security guard or the janitor when they left the building. Maybe his own talkative deputy leaked the news, he thought.

"And you have some information you think could be helpful to us?"

Heather's artfully rouged cheeks grew even rosier as she began, excitedly nodding her head. "Oh, yes, I think so. I'm in Lichner's ancient history class, and there's this guy who's been getting really bad grades. I mean, nobody is doing really well in the class, but Matt—that's his name—he hasn't gotten one passing grade yet."

Browning interrupted. "How would you know this?"

She narrowed her eyes and leaned forward. "Because

he's always complaining about Lichner and how unfair he is. We were talking about today's test before class, and Matt said he's gotten all Fs on everything he's done. He said he hates Lichner and probably has to take a summer class to make up this credit if he fails. I think he's supposed to graduate with his two-year associate's degree this semester."

The information was useful but not startling. Browning figured the same circumstance could apply to several of the professor's other students. It was worth checking out though.

"You know Matt's last name, Heather?"

She smiled again when he said her name. "Yes. It's Baker. We both went to Hillcrest High School. I think he still lives in town."

Browning nodded and wrote in his notebook, then flipped it shut. "Thanks for the information. We'll follow up on it. Be sure to let us know if you think of something else that might be helpful." He gave her an obligatory smile.

She touched his arm as he turned away, anxiously stepping toward him.

"Um, Sheriff, you know, I could help you out by . . . I don't know . . . maybe calling Matt and trying to get some information out of him. I think he kind of likes me, so he might tell me something that he won't tell you."

Trying to dismiss her as quickly as possible, Browning held up his hand as he backed away.

"That won't be necessary, Heather. Thanks anyway.

Good-bye now," he said turning away from her. He couldn't see the disappointed look on her face when he rejected her offer, but Sarah didn't miss it from her vantage point down the hallway.

"Haven't you left yet?" Browning asked her, not attempting to hide the exasperation in his voice. "Time to leave—now! This is a crime scene, Sarah."

"I know. That's why I'm here. Wow, that girl really has the hots for you!"

Browning feigned disagreement. He didn't want to admit to his fiancée that he also recognized Heather's obvious infatuation with him.

"Who, Miss Bergen? She's just a kid with a fascination for detective work, that's all."

Sarah smiled at his discomfort.

"Mmm. Girls don't look adoringly at the local sheriff just because they admire his law enforcement skills. I can attest to that. I'm betting this won't be the last time the 'kid' remembers some information she just has to share with you." Sarah laughed, feeling a slight pang of jealousy.

Firmly but tenderly, Browning gripped Sarah's shoulders and turned her toward the doorway.

"And if she does, that won't be any business of yours. Now, I'm going to stand here and watch you walk out that door—and enjoy the view, by the way—so we can do our work without the press hanging around, okay?"

Sarah walked slowly as his hands guided her out.

"I'm leaving—not because you told me to, but because I'm on deadline. Be prepared to answer several questions tomorrow morning, Sheriff."

Then, making sure no one was near, she quickly brushed his lips with hers and whispered, "I love you."

Browning returned to the classroom as the ambulance crew was zipping the body bag holding Professor Lichner's corpse. Barone was finishing up his collection of evidence.

"We're almost finished here," Thompson told him, looking at his notes. "I've talked to the janitor and a couple of curious teachers who managed to slip in a rear door of the building. They didn't give me too much to go on, but one mentioned we might want to talk to the school board president, Beth Callison. I guess they were pretty close."

Browning nodded, watching the paramedics lift the bundled body on to a gurney.

"We've got a small crowd gathered outside the building, Charlie, and who knows what kind of media has shown up. Let's help our guys give the body an escort to the ambulance, and then we can take a look-see at the people in the crowd too. You know, check out any weirdos."

Thompson smirked. "We're on a college campus, Sheriff. This place is crawling with weirdos."

Browning laughed. "You're still trapped in the sixties and seventies, Charlie. There are no more hippies. Oh, and I've been meaning to tell you that leisure suits have been out of style for a while too."

Thompson grunted something unintelligible and the two men watched the ambulance crew wedge the gurney out the classroom doorway and into the hallway. A deputy standing guard at the building exit held the door open for them as the crowd pressed closer.

"Everyone back, please!" a deputy shouted to the onlookers, who obediently parted to open a path for the deceased. A woman looked at the body bag and gasped, covering her mouth with her hand and turning away.

Browning noticed a man coming from the direction of the administration building, walking quickly and then breaking into a jog as the gurney reached the ambulance. He headed directly for them, his red tie blowing over the shoulder of his white dress shirt as he hopped over puddles. When he tried to muscle his way between the paramedics for a look at the body, Browning grabbed his arm and held him back.

"Excuse me, sir. You need to step back."

Flustered, the man ran his fingers through his thick, wavy brown hair, straining to look into the ambulance.

"I heard that it's Philip . . . Professor Lichner," he said between gulps of air, then looked at Browning for the first time. "You're the sheriff, aren't you? I met you when you taught here. I work here too. Is it true? Is it Philip?"

Browning took the man by the arm again, gently this

time, and led him to the sidewalk, away from ambulance and the crowd. Thompson followed.

"Did you know Professor Lichner well?" Browning asked.

The man held his stomach and his head dropped. "Oh, my God. It *is* Philip, isn't it? What happened?"

"We're not sure yet, but if you knew him, we'd appreciate any information you can give us—any recent problems, anyone giving him a hard time lately, things like that. Was he a friend?"

The man put his hands on his hips and breathed deeply, trying to recover from his jog as well as the painful news.

"More of a work friend than a personal friend, I guess you can say. Still, this is such a shock. I just saw him this morning."

Thompson took a toothpick out of his mouth. "What's your name, sir?"

The man, whom Browning guessed to be in his mid-thirties, loosened his tie. "Tom Barrett. I work in the bursar's office."

"The what?" Thompson asked, furrowing his brow.

"It's like the school's financial office, Charlie," Browning interjected. "All the accounting is done there. Has Professor Lichner had any problems that you know of with anyone, Tom?"

Barrett shook his head slowly, staring at the ground. "No, but we didn't talk about things like that. It was mostly, 'Hey, how're you doing, how's your new class—stuff like that.'"

Thompson scratched his head. "Then how come you ran over here so upset if you didn't really know him that well, sir?"

Barrett snapped his head toward Thompson. "How would you feel if a co-worker was murdered? Nothing like this ever happens on campus. You don't have to know him well to be shocked by it. Like I said, I just saw him this morning and he seemed fine. This is unbelievable."

Thompson glanced at his notes. "Who did the deceased hang out with, do you know? Did he have any close friends you're aware of?"

Barrett watched as the ambulance's red lights began to flash and the vehicle slowly pulled away from the crowd, heading toward Doc Fellows' office, then turned his attention back to Thompson.

"Some of the professors in the history department are pretty tight—I don't know if Philip was part of that group. Oh, and I used to see him on campus a lot with Beth Callison—she's the school board president. I'd see them together in the cafeteria quite often, having lunch or whatever."

"*Used* to see them?" Browning asked. "They stopped associating?"

Barrett shrugged. "I don't know the details. Like I said, we were only acquaintances."

Thompson fished a stick of gum from his shirt pocket and began to unwrap it with his teeth. "I'm guessing there's a lot of gossip around a college campus, Mr.

Barrett," he mumbled as he spat the wrapper on to the ground. "You're telling me you've heard nothing about the relationship between one of the professors and the school board president?"

"I said that I knew they were seeing each other, and then I heard she was really upset when they split up, but I didn't ask any questions," Barrett said, annoyed. "I'm really not interested in the soap operas that occur around here."

Thompson popped his gum. "Do you know of anyone who might have wanted to harm the professor?"

Barrett shook his head and put his hands on his hips. "Really, I barely knew the man. Maybe you should talk to Beth Callison. I'm sure she'd know a lot more about Philip than I do."

Browning could hear the rising irritation in Barrett's voice, a frequent reaction in even the most cooperative witnesses when subjected to Thompson's persistent and often abrasive questioning. It wasn't the kind of interviewing style that Browning particularly liked, but Thompson had become his best detective using it. Still, he decided, they could always get back to Barrett later if necessary.

"Well, thanks for your help, Tom," Browning said. "Give us a call if you think of anything else that might be helpful."

Barrett nodded. "I will. I hope you get the guy. I don't think any of us will feel comfortable around here until there's an arrest."

Some onlookers still stood in small groups, excitedly discussing the news, while others returned to their previous business. Thompson and Browning watched as some approached Barrett, probably asking him what the police had said.

"Looks like we need to talk to Beth Callison ASAP, huh?" Thompson said. "She's probably here somewhere. Wasn't there a school board meeting tonight?"

Browning wiped his forehead with his sleeve as a light mist began to fall again. "Yeah. I'm going to make sure we're all finished in the classroom. Why don't you try to find her and give me a call on my cell if you do."

Thompson started heading toward the administration building.

"And, hey, Charlie," Browning called to him, pointing to the gum wrapper on the ground. "Pick that up, wouldja? Don't you know there's a fine for littering?"

He smiled and turned, leaving Thompson to roll his eyes and stuff the wrapper in his pocket.

Sarah ran from her pickup truck to her front porch, bounding up the three stairs to avoid a complete drenching from the rain that had turned into a full-fledged thunderstorm. She had stopped in at the newspaper office to rearrange the layout for the next issue, opening a prime front page space for the murder story. It would be written the next morning after getting what she hoped would be last-minute details from Mark. A photo of the shrouded body being wheeled from the building would run with it.

Sarah was hungry. She'd eaten only a bowl of cereal for dinner, saving room for her recently postponed encounter with a huge hot fudge sundae that night. She and Mark, as usual, would have to reschedule that date. She popped a bagel in the toaster and grabbed a jar of strawberry jelly from the refrigerator.

Oh, well. Probably better for my waistline if I still want to fit into my wedding dress in three months.

She gobbled the bagel and washed it down with a small glass of milk, thinking about the dress. She had chosen the first one she'd tried on, a sleeveless ivory satin with a fitted empire waist. Like the wedding she and Mark were planning, the design was simple. In fact, it wasn't even an "official" wedding dress—she'd found it in the prom dress section of the department store. Choosing the dress was easy—deciding what kind of veil to wear wasn't. She'd probably looked at a hundred different kinds.

As a bride and bridegroom well into their thirties, they'd decided to forego the expensive wedding reception traditions and focus their attention and funds on improvements needed at the lake house. Following the church ceremony, close friends and family would return to the house for the reception. Although she tried to envision a reception on the beach side of the house, Sarah knew that wedding guests probably wouldn't tolerate sand between their toes. Instead, they would put a party tent on the street side of the cottage, where the front lawn was huge and sported enough soft grass to make it workable.

She drifted into the bedroom, wedding plans still on her mind, and took her dress out of the closet. Lifting the plastic covering and hooking the hanger on the door top, she stood back and gazed at the gown. *Maybe just a short wisp of veiling attached to the back of a simple head wreath of flowers would be best. Or maybe just the wreath alone would be better.* She frowned as the choices began to multiply.

Her deliberations were interrupted by the sound of a thump on her front porch.

"Mark?" she called, knowing the sound of her voice would easily penetrate her drafty windows. She listened for the sound of his key in her door, surprised that he was able to break away so soon from the murder case, and anxious to wrap her arms around him.

Heading into the living room, she heard another thump on the stairs and wondered if Mark was returning to his car for something. She went to the window that looked out on the driveway and drew back the lace curtain, peering into the darkness outside.

As her eyes adjusted to the dim light provided by a full moon, she saw a clump of beach grasses next to the drive bending and swaying as if something had just passed through them. Her pickup was the only vehicle parked outside.

She walked over to the window off the porch and looked outside, seeing nothing but the two Adirondack chairs.

She assured herself that it was probably an animal, knowing that raccoons were frequent visitors to beach houses in their quests for food. She made a mental note to make sure her garbage can lids were tightly shut when she left for work in the morning.

Sarah sat on her blue denim couch and pulled her feet up under her, switching on the television and wondering if the Traverse City news stations would have a report on the murder. She knew she'd have trouble going to sleep until she got her "good night" call from Mark.

And the strange noise on her porch was still on her mind.

Chapter Four

Only a few concerned taxpayers remained in the school board's meeting room as members wrapped up their session in a hurry. Word had spread inside the administration building that someone had been murdered on campus, sending most of the audience rushing to the scene and drawing the curiosity of board members as well. They quickly agreed to postpone further discussion on issues until the next meeting. A murder was much more interesting.

Browning and Thompson stood in the back of the room, watching Beth Callison gather up the plentiful paperwork in front of her and stuffing it in her soft leather briefcase. Her slender hands shook as she reached for the documents and stored them away, then tucked stray locks of auburn hair behind an ear. She nodded when a fellow board member whispered to her, never raising her head as she looked down at her briefcase.

"I'll be fine," she said in a strangled voice, loud enough for the detectives to hear. "Thank you for your concern."

The board member briefly touched her shoulder and turned to leave the room, eyeing Browning and Thompson with curiosity as he walked out the door. Callison grabbed her briefcase, squeezed her eyes shut and breathed a heavy sigh. Composing herself and opening her eyes, she saw the two men.

"Is this in regard to Philip?" she immediately asked.

A navy-blue skirt suit clung to every curve of her sturdy frame, an outfit probably purchased before putting on recent weight. Her brown eyes were overpowered by dark circles beneath, but they hinted that this woman, probably in her late thirties, was intelligent as well as attractive. She stood stiffly behind the board's dais.

Browning moved closer to her before speaking, not wanting his voice to carry into the ears of passersby in the hallway.

"I'm Sheriff Browning and this is Detective Thompson. You heard about Professor Lichner, Ms. Callison?"

Her eyes grew moist, but her voice was steady. "I know who you are, Sheriff. We've met before—I'm the director of the Hillcrest Public Library. My position on the school board is voluntary."

She continued, quickly catching a tear with her little finger before it escaped the corner of one eye. "One of our security guards delivered the news to us during our meeting break. The entire board is already aware of it. Who did this to him?"

Browning looked back at Thompson, still standing near the door. "Charlie, shut the door, please." He pointed to another door in the corner of the room behind the dais. "Is that a conference room, Ms. Callison? Would you mind talking to us for a moment in there?"

She hesitated, looking at a round clock on the wall. "I really would prefer to do that at another time," she said, closing her eyes and pressing a finger to her temple. "This has been quite a shock, and I also need to speak tonight with several college administrators concerning this . . . tragedy."

She began to walk toward the outer door, brushing past Browning and stopping abruptly when Thompson blocked her path.

"We know you were close to the victim, ma'am," Browning said. "It's important that we talk to you. Now."

She tossed her hair back and allowed a small laugh to escape. "Isn't this a bit heavy-handed, Sheriff?" She looked at the immovable Thompson. "Not allowing me to leave? Someone in my position certainly shouldn't be treated like this, but if you simply cannot schedule another time to meet with me, I suppose I can spare a few minutes."

Her low-heeled black pumps clicked on the linoleum floor as she quickly headed into the conference room.

"Let's go talk to Miss High-and-Mighty," Thompson grumbled as he scratched his stomach.

Callison was seated at the head of the conference table, fingers drumming its surface. "As I said, I don't have a lot of time and I really don't think I have information that would be helpful to you."

Browning sat in the chair to her side, watching as she took her still-quivering hand off the table and rested it in her lap. Thompson sat across from Browning.

"What was your relationship with Professor Lichner, ma'am?" Browning asked.

She cleared her throat. "We dated for a while. Nothing serious. It was only for a few months until we . . . just lost interest, I guess you could say. We both have . . . I mean . . . *had* busy schedules and it just didn't work out. I'm divorced and don't want another dead-end relationship. We ended it about two months ago."

She looked at Thompson when his gum loudly popped.

"So you're saying this was a mutual decision, to stop seeing each other? We've heard that you were upset about the breakup," he said.

She quickly looked down at her lap and smoothed her skirt. "It was definitely mutual, and any rumors that you heard to the contrary are simply false. Why does any of this matter? Are you insinuating that I—"

Browning shook his hand and waved his hand. "We're just gathering all the information we can about the professor, Ms. Callison. Do you know of anyone who might have wanted to harm him, or anybody he's been having problems with?"

"Problems? Well, of course, teachers are always having all sorts of problems with their students—Philip, in particular. I told him that I felt he was too demanding of his students. This is a community college, not Harvard University. Many of his students were failing, and I know of at least one that made repeated and unpleasant visits to his office begging him to give him a break with his grades."

Browning leaned forward. "Any chance you might remember the name of that student?"

"Oh, he would never mention complete names, but I believe it was something like Mike, or Matt. Philip believed in keeping information like that confidential. He was quite close-mouthed about such things, almost to the point of refusing to discuss any of our common school experiences. That probably added to the problems with our relationship. I'm guessing the student was in one of his ancient history classes, though, because he briefly mentioned it just before we stopped seeing each other. That's what he's teaching this semester."

"Did he say why the student's visits to his office were unpleasant?" Browning asked.

She pursed her lips in thought. "I remember he mentioned that the young man began crying at one point and Philip felt very uncomfortable. That's about it."

Thompson began picking dirt from beneath his thumb's fingernail. "You said his reluctance to talk about such things added to the problems with your relationship," he said, examining his nail. "What other problems did you have, ma'am?"

She sat up straight and folded her arms. "I already

told you—busy schedules, lack of enthusiasm for the relationship, poor communication—the normal problems. Nothing that would prompt me to murder him, Detective," she said in a sarcastic tone.

"How about other people in his life?" Browning said. "Who else was he close to?"

She looked at her watch and exhaled loudly in a dramatic show of impatience. "I can't really say that Philip was close to anyone," she said in a clipped voice. "He was never married, and his father is the only family he has left—his mother died some years ago. Other than mentioning that his father resides in a retirement home in Milwaukee, Philip rarely spoke of him."

Thompson interrupted. "We've already contacted Milwaukee police and they'll do the death notification, boss. Lichner had family information in his wallet."

Callison put her hands on the table and started to push her chair back. "Is that all, gentlemen? I really must speak to the administrators."

Browning put his hand on her arm. "Just a few more questions and you'll be free to go," he said firmly. "How about close friends? There must have been other people in his life."

She gripped the edge of the table, feet flat on the floor, obvious that she planned to stand and leave in a moment. "Casual acquaintances, all from the school. You know, he'd be invited to an occasional wedding, a surprise birthday party, that sort of thing. But I don't recall him ever inviting someone to go out for a drink or watch a football game or whatever. In fact, I only saw one other person at his house during the time we were dating, and that was Tom Barrett. He works in our bursar's office."

Thompson stopped chewing his gum. "And what was Mr. Barrett doing at the professor's house, do you know?"

She waved her hand. "It wasn't a personal visit. He was leaving as I was arriving, and he said he needed to drop off some paperwork for Philip. That's all. Now, I really must go."

Browning looked at Thompson and nodded, a signal that they'd let her leave. She looked at her watch once again and stood, picking up her briefcase.

"Perhaps I will think of something else that might be helpful to you when this all sinks in. I just hope there's not some nut loose on campus, but that seems to be the only explanation for Philip's death."

The detectives said nothing as she left the room and waited for the sound of her heels to fade as she headed into the hallway.

"Being a former girlfriend of the guy, she sure didn't sound too upset about his sudden demise," Thompson observed.

Browning leaned back in his chair and clasped his hands behind his head. "Yeah, she was kind of cold, wasn't she? Maybe it's just her personality. We should probably talk to some of her co-workers to take a better look at her. I'd like to know how she *really* felt about the breakup with the good professor."

He stood and put his hands on his hips, arching his back to stretch the knotted muscles there. "How about we call it a night, Charlie, and start over again in the morning? Maybe Doc Fellows will work late tonight and have some postmortem results for us then."

Sarah clicked off the TV and looked at the phone. Mark hadn't called yet, and she figured he was still working the murder case at the college. The Traverse City stations had headlined it in their Breaking News segment, but few details were given. Reporters had arrived at the scene well after Lichner's body had been removed and the only information police had provided was that a professor had been found dead under suspicious circumstances. Sarah smiled at that, knowing Mark had directed his deputies to keep their mouths shut.

She padded across the old Oriental rug that covered the pine plank floor in her living room—one of only four rooms in her cottage along with the kitchen, bedroom and a tiny bathroom—and looked out the window. The sky had cleared after the earlier rain, and the full moon was even brighter than when she heard the noise on her porch. She had hoped to see Mark's unmarked squad car making its way down her gravel driveway, but no such luck. It was quiet outside.

She knew the noise had to be a raccoon and tried to remember if she secured the lid on her outdoor garbage can when she opened it the day before. The last thing she wanted to do before heading to work in the morning was to clean up a week's worth of rotting food and empty containers that might have been scattered on the sand by a hungry animal. She grabbed a flashlight from a drawer in her roll-top desk and decided to investigate then rather than wait until morning. Slipping into a pair of beach shoes she kept near the door, she unlocked the dead bolt and headed outside.

An outside wall lantern immediately illuminated a white envelope on the porch.

That explained the noise, Sarah figured.

Puzzled, she reached down for the envelope while her eyes swept the area around her house. The moonlight revealed nothing suspicious, but the shadowed areas near the beach grasses and small trees raised goosebumps on her arms. Flicking on the flashlight, she swept the beam from side to side and saw nothing out of the ordinary. She hurried back into the house, just a bit relieved.

She tossed the flashlight on the couch and, still standing by the door, tore open the envelope. She was too curious to sit down before removing its contents.

Inside was a letter-sized piece of common printer paper with an obviously computer-generated message.

A newspaper editor shouldn't marry a sheriff. Readers and voters won't like it.

"Oh, jeez," Sarah groaned, finally sinking onto the couch and reading the note again. She rubbed her forehead and slowly shook her head. It was the first time she'd received any kind of negative comment regarding her engagement to Mark since he ran for election the year before. Some people, including *Times* publisher Vernon

Jakes, were concerned that the newspaper couldn't objectively cover the crime and politics of the sheriff's department when the editor was marrying the head honcho. But after the heat of the election, the rhetoric had died down. She'd also convinced her publisher that she could keep her private and professional lives separate.

This was different than receiving a complaining phone call at the office or a letter to the editor. Someone was so incensed by the relationship that he or she drove to her fairly remote location, twenty minutes outside of town, to send a message loud and clear. A slight shiver sent Sarah reaching for the throw blanket on the back of her couch, and then, the phone.

Mark picked up after the first ring. "Hi, hon," he said warmly. "I just stepped in the door."

His voice calmed her normally steady nerves that had been rattled by the unexpectedly close delivery of an angry reader's opinion. "Hey, how'd it go tonight?" She didn't want to come on like a damsel in distress, although she was feeling quite distressed at the moment.

He laughed. "Is that a reporter's way of saying, 'Who'd you talk to and what did you find out?'"

She managed to chuckle. "No, I'll wait until tomorrow morning to interrogate you. I just needed to call you now because . . . well, you know how I sleep better when I talk to you before going to bed and, well . . . you hadn't called yet and—"

"What's wrong?" he asked, hearing a tone in her voice that told him something was amiss.

"Oh, it's nothing, really," she said in a failed effort to sound convincing. "Some wacko just decided to mysteriously deliver a complaint letter to the editor's house rather than through the normal post office channels. And, it concerns you and me."

Browning was silent for a moment. "He showed up at the house? Did you let him in?"

"No, it wasn't like that. I heard a noise on the porch earlier tonight and I thought it was a raccoon or another animal looking for food. So, I went outside a few minutes ago to make sure my garbage can lid was on tight, and I found this letter sitting in front of the door." She read it to him.

"Idiot," Browning said under his breath. "Some people just can't let it go, even after all these months. I'm sure that's the last you'll hear from him."

Sarah stood up and walked to the door, locking the deadbolt and doorknob. "I know. It was just so weird that it kind of shook me up a little. I mean, why would this be so important to someone that they'd sneak a letter to my house? And how do they know where I live?"

He snorted. "Sarah, you wouldn't believe all the political hijinks I've had to put up with since becoming sheriff. Take it from me—this is probably just another ploy that some potential opponent is pulling more than three years before the next election. They're trying to get me to reconsider the possibility of running again, and they figure one way to do that is to scare you."

She rubbed her forehead. "It's not so much that it scares me, Mark. I just can't lose my credibility with my readers. That's very important to me, and this letter might say what a lot of readers are feeling."

He hesitated before responding. "So, are you changing your mind about marrying me, kiddo?" he said, only half-joking.

"You know I'd never change my mind. You're stuck with me. And you're probably right—it's just someone trying to throw a wrench in your political career."

Browning sighed. "It's too bad that politics comes with the job. I'm not too good at that game, but I'll play it if I have to. You know how much I'd like to change things in the sheriff's department."

Sarah smiled. "You already have, and you're doing a great job. Of course, the department's media relations could use some improvement."

"Yeah? Well, I think my relations with a certain member of the media are pretty fantastic, don't you?" He laughed.

Sarah looked at the photo she kept of him on her desk, taken by her when they visited Mackinac Island the summer before. A wide smile dimpled his cheek and his dark eyes, framed in black lashes, were filled with the love he felt for the photographer.

"Yes, they are," she whispered, then added quickly, "Does that mean you'll answer a couple of questions I have?"

"Not now! You said you'd wait until tomorrow!"

She considered that, but she'd also discovered from past experience that Mark was more talkative in the relaxed atmosphere of his apartment than in the high-pressure surroundings of his office. He was always smart enough to preface his remarks with, 'This is off the record,' but even unprintable remarks could point her in the right direction for a good story.

"I'm just wondering about what the blond girl said— that there was a student Lichner had trouble with. Did you talk to the student?"

"We talked to a few people tonight. I'm not telling you who, and we don't consider anyone a suspect. That's all you need to know for now."

Sarah persisted. "How about the weapon? Was he shot, stabbed, killed with something else?"

Browning hooted. "You must think I really do a super job if you expect me to know the details of death already, Sarah. If we're lucky, Doc will have some results from the post tomorrow, but don't count on it. Hey you, let's drop this murder talk and change the subject to something more pleasant, like how much I love you and how I hope you sleep tight tonight."

She relented, his soothing voice convincing her to forget the events of the day and escape to some much-needed slumber. "Okay, but I'll be checking with you in the morning before my deadline to see if there's anything new to report. And, I love you too."

She changed into a pair of cotton pajama pants and a white T-shirt. Pulling back her down blanket and crawling under the sheet, she gazed out her window at the gigantic moon, thinking about the strange letter.

She was still thinking about it an hour later.

Chapter Five

Doc Fellows awoke Browning with a 5:30 A.M. phone call. He'd worked long into the night on the autopsy, and his report was ready. They decided to meet at the sheriff's department in two hours, so Browning made wakeup calls to Thompson and evidence technician Barone, telling them to be there.

The three men were waiting in the conference room, huddled over cups of black coffee and stifling yawns when Fellows entered. He was whistling as he adjusted a bow tie with one hand and held a file folder close to his chest with the other.

"How do you do it, Doc?" asked a bleary-eyed Thompson. "You got to be thirty years older than the rest of us, you worked all night, and you look fresh as a damn daisy."

The lanky doctor smiled as he took a seat and withdrew papers from the envelope. "I get plenty of sleep being retired from regular practice, fellas. And the beauty of being medical examiner of Potter County is that there's not much work for me. Keeps my mind alert, though."

He licked a finger and paged through his reports, double-checking the information and nodding to himself. Then he raised his head and looked at the investigators, a smile breaking across his face.

"Good news, boys," he told them with a wink.

Browning rubbed his eyes with two hands, trying to wipe away his fatigue. "You arrested the killer? Great. Let's go home."

Fellows chuckled. "Well, maybe not that good, but it will help you. Take a look at this."

He withdrew a white envelope from his packet and carefully unfolded the piece of paper within, setting it gently on the table in front of them. The men all leaned forward, narrowing their eyes to get a closer look at the object, no more than an inch long, lying on top of it.

"It's the tip of a knife," Thompson said. "Nice work, Doc."

Barone half-stood, bending over the table and the silver point of the knife, studying it with an expert eye.

"You'll want to put that in your evidence file, Joe," Fellows said. "That's from the knife that killed Professor Lichner, God rest his soul. You find the knife that matches that and it might lead you to the killer."

Browning began to roll up the sleeves of his blue button-down shirt. "Tell us all about it, Doc."

Adjusting the eyeglasses that had slipped down his nose, Fellows began his report. "I'll just give you the essentials here. The professor was murdered with one thrust of a knife, probably with a blade measuring seven inches long judging by the size of the broken portion and width of the wound. It severed the major nerve centers in his spine, where the blade broke on bone and then punctured a portion of his heart. It was a highly efficient attack, but probably just a lucky one, if you will."

"Was death immediate?" Browning asked.

Fellows nodded. "The destruction of his nerve center rendered him helpless and led to the cessation of all vital functions. That's why there was no sign of a struggle at the scene. The injury to the heart was just icing on the cake for our murderer. The poor man had no defense and never saw it coming."

Thompson was rubbing his chin, taking in the information. "What was the time of death, Doc?"

Fellows turned a few pages in his report. "I would estimate it to be about an hour before the body was found, which was eight o'clock in the evening, correct?" He looked at the investigators for confirmation. "So, he died around seven that night."

He reached into his folders, took out photographs of the body, taken during the autopsy, and passed them to Browning.

"You'll see photos of the wound in there, Mark," Fellows said. "It tells me that your murderer is probably right-handed because the blade entered the professor's back just to the right of the spine and then angled slightly left. It would be difficult for a left-handed person to perform such a maneuver."

Browning studied the photos. Despite having seen hundreds like them in his years of experience, it was never a sight he could get used to.

"The angle of attack—what does it say about the killer's height, Doc?" he asked.

Fellows shrugged his shoulders. "Not much, Mark. Professor Lichner was about five-foot, ten-inches tall. The knife entered his body after a downward thrust. Someone taller probably wouldn't raise the knife too high before hitting down. A shorter person might raise his arm higher to strike down. Point is, the knife would end up in the same area regardless of the attacker's height. Sorry, can't help you out there."

Browning stood, mimicking the action of a knife attack against an invisible victim. "I'm wondering how strong a person would have to be to knife someone hard enough to break off part of the weapon. What do you think, Doc? Would it have to be a pretty strong guy?"

Fellows shook his head. "Not an Arnold Schwarzenegger, if that's what you're asking. A sharp knife penetrates tissue fairly easily, and a thin blade like this one wouldn't need too much force to break off when contacting bone. Anyone in fairly good shape with an extra shot of adrenaline, man or woman, could have done this."

Browning picked up the piles of photos and tossed them to Thompson, who took a quick look, grimaced and shoved them down the table to Barone. He took his ever-present wad of gum from his mouth and tossed it in a nearby wastebasket.

"Here are a few other details on the body, gentlemen. The professor was a heavy smoker—I'd give him only a few more years before those dirty lungs of his gave him some nasty trouble. I also noticed that his fingernails were chewed to the quick and his cuticles looked like he picked at them constantly. Must've been a nervous sort."

Further information on the corpse would be available, Fellows told them, when the results of the blood test came back from the state crime lab.

"So, unless you need me for anything else, sirs, I'm off for a breakfast of scrambled eggs and bacon followed by a long nap." He smoothed his still-full head of white hair as he headed for the door.

It was time to hear Barone's report. Thompson and Browning had scoured the scene with him, and they knew there was little evidence to collect.

"Hair, fibers and fingerprints is pretty much all we have to work with, guys," he lamented. "And do you know how much hair I had to collect in a room where college girls groom themselves before the start of each class? I have hair coming out of my ears . . . er, pardon the pun."

Browning tapped his fingers on the table. "Crime lab will take at least a week to classify everything, right, Joe? Sounds like we have nothing that could lead us to the killer. All we have is evidence to confirm that a suspect we may or may not find was in the room at some time."

"Exactly," Barone agreed. "And if we do take someone into custody, it's likely there won't be any blood evidence on discarded or even washed clothing because there was no evidence of spatters. The only blood in the room was pooled on the floor after he hemorrhaged. And I found nothing unusual in the room. I'm guessing the guy walked in, didn't touch a thing, stabbed Lichner, and left the room. Not much evidence to work with."

Browning turned to Thompson. "We've got a missing weapon. Are our deputies done with the campus search yet?"

"Nah, they ended it last night when it got too dark," Thompson answered. "All the buildings were searched, but we've got some of the outside areas to finish up. They should be out there as we speak. I can't believe no one saw a guy walking around with a seven-inch knife."

Browning shrugged. "The security guard said most of the classes were over and the campus was pretty deserted. Plus, the killer could have concealed it somehow."

He continued. "So, let's talk about who we want to focus on, Charlie. Nobody stands out at the moment, but I think we should check out his students today—see who was failing or doing poorly in his class."

Thompson nodded. "And I'd like to take another

look at Beth Callison, boss. Her demeanor just didn't sit right with me. Plus, I think we need to talk to Tom Barrett again. He said he didn't know Lichner well, but he was seen at his house."

Browning pulled a pen from his shirt pocket. "Let's see," he said, scribbling on a notebook in front of him. "Death occurred around seven P.M. and the board meeting began at seven-thirty. That would've given her plenty of time to kill him and get back for the meeting. We should talk to her colleagues to see how long she was in the building before the meeting started. We know Barrett was on campus when the body was found. We need to check on his whereabouts too."

Thompson scratched his cheek. "How about her motive? A woman scorned?"

Browning threw up his hands. "Could be. We have to learn more about their relationship."

Barone stood. "I find all of this fascinating, gentlemen, but I have some work to do. I'll get back to you when the reports come in on our evidence, or lack thereof."

He was leaving just as the department's receptionist, Jean, knocked on the conference room door, telling Browning he had a visitor who said she had urgent information regarding the murder.

"Her name is Heather Bergen," the receptionist said.

Browning heaved a sigh, mumbling, "Fine. Have her wait in my office."

Thompson noted the sheriff's less-than-enthusiastic reaction. "You know her?"

"She's the one I told you about who gave me Matt Baker's name—the student who's failing Lichner's class."

A look of amusement passed over Thompson's face. "Oh, yeah—the cute blond kid who was following you around like a puppy dog yesterday. Looks like you got yourself a fan."

Browning was sporting a sour face as he and Thompson headed down the hall. "You should sit in on this, Charlie. She's a pain in the neck, but her information's pretty good."

Thompson feigned a pout. "I feel bad. How come you get an admirer and I don't? Is it my breath?"

Browning shoved an elbow into his detective's ribs before entering his office. Heather sat in one of the two visitors' chairs across from Browning's desk, her crossed legs exposed by an ultra-short jean skirt topped with a tight red Hillcrest College T-shirt. Her smile faded when she saw Thompson walk in the door.

"Hello, Heather," the sheriff said in a business-like tone, nodding to her as he took a seat. Thompson sat in the chair next to her. "This is Detective Thompson. You have some information for us?"

She looked askance at Thompson. "I wanted to talk to *you*, Sheriff. I don't think *he* needs to be here, does he?"

Browning saw a smile playing on Thompson's lips. "This is the lead detective on the case, Heather, so it is very important for him to hear your information. That's why you're here, isn't it?"

She looked surprised. "The lead detective? I thought *you* are the lead detective!"

Browning shook his head. "I'm assisting Detective Thompson since this is a unique case, but my responsibilities as sheriff limit the amount of time I can spend on it. I want you to contact Charlie if you have anything to tell us in the future, okay?"

Heather tossed her head back. "I really would rather talk to you, Sheriff. I know you better. And I think I could be really helpful."

Thompson was leaning an elbow on the chair's armrest, hiding a smile behind his hand and looking at Browning with crinkled eyes. "It's okay if she'd rather talk to you, boss. I don't mind."

Not amused, Browning shot his detective a look. "No, Charlie. She will talk to *you*." He turned to Heather. "Now, what do you have to tell us?"

Displeased with the decision, Heather folded her arms and looked down at the floor before reluctantly answering. "Well, I remembered something Matt Baker told me about his father. I guess he promised Matt a lot of money if he makes it through Hillcrest College and gets his two-year associate's degree. Matt was bragging about what he was going to do with the money, like buy a new car and stuff. If he doesn't graduate, he won't get the money. That might be why he killed Professor Lichner, right?"

Browning and Thompson exchanged a quick look. "How much money is his father going to give him?" Thompson asked.

Heather looked at the detective with distaste, her eyes moving from his scuffed wing tip shoes to his gravy-stained tie. "He wouldn't say, but with all the things Matt said he was going to buy, I'm guessing thousands and thousands of dollars. Matt's father owns a big marina in Franklin and he wants Matt to get more education so he can take over the business some day."

Browning made a connection. "Baker's Marina? That's his dad's business?" He turned to Thompson. "Charlie, this is the Baker kid. You know who I mean?"

"Yeah, gotcha," Thompson answered with a raised eyebrow.

Heather didn't miss the exchanged looks. "I know what you're thinking," she said with self-satisfaction. "Matt's been in trouble in the past, and you're thinking he might be in trouble again, right?"

"What have you heard about Matt's past, Heather?" Browning asked.

She rolled her eyes. "Gosh, what *haven't* I heard? Matt practically brags about the stuff he's done. He's almost, like, proud of it! I know he got caught doing a couple of burglaries and everyone knows he was suspended for a while in high school because he was selling pot."

Browning leaned forward. "Has he been doing any bragging lately about bad things he's done?"

Heather grew more animated. "No, but like I told you last night, I'm sure I could get him talking if you want me to spend some time with him. He's got such a big mouth and he's always trying to impress me talking about the things he does. I *know* I could get him to confess to the murder if you'll let me work with you on this."

As tempting as the idea was, Browning immediately decided not to let this young girl become involved in the case before they had exhausted all other means of investigation. He and Thompson hadn't even talked to Baker yet. But it wasn't a bad idea to keep this option open.

"First of all, Heather, Matt is not a suspect at this time," he said. "Keep your eyes and ears open, but for now, I'm asking you to stay away from Matt and let us handle this. Do you understand that?"

She nodded eagerly, standing to leave and feeling pacified with the belief that Browning would need her assistance soon. She knew they wouldn't get any information out of Matt.

He walked her to the reception area of the department, where he saw Sarah stepping up to the bulletproof glass that separated it from the public lobby. She spotted him and smiled, giving a small wave.

"Go ahead and let her in, Jean," he called to the receptionist. A buzzer sounded and Sarah opened the security door.

"Hey, you," he said in a gentle voice that put a slight frown on Heather's face as she brushed past Sarah and out the door. "I get a personal visit rather than a phone call, huh?"

Sarah turned to watch Heather leave the building. "Wow, she's here bright and early. Must've had something pretty important to tell you."

Browning put his hand on Sarah's back and directed her toward his office. "Nothing we couldn't have found out on our own—and nothing that the newspaper needs to know about."

He sat at his desk and Sarah perched on its edge, notebook in her lap. "I figured I'd just stop on the way to the paper and get the new details on the case," she said, looking at the papers on his desk and employing her highly honed ability to read important documents upside down.

"I know what you're doing, Sarah," Browning smiled, gathering up the autopsy reports and putting them in his drawer. "Knock it off."

She jotted some notes on the pad. "So, he was stabbed in the back with a seven-inch knife. You guys find the weapon yet?"

Browning winced. He'd rather she not know the details about the knife. If it became public, the bad guy would surely permanently dispose of the weapon if he hadn't done so already. It was best to keep the murderer in the dark about what they knew.

"Listen, hon, I can't tell you what to print, but revealing the information on the weapon could really hurt the investigation. Could we compromise on this?"

Sarah never intended to print the detail about the size

of the knife—she knew it could impede a police investigation and that wasn't her goal. It was the compromise she was angling for.

She pretended to make a concession. "Well . . . I guess I don't need to report the size of the weapon if you can give me some other information that's worthwhile. And I don't mean something like, 'We are interviewing people of interest and the investigation is continuing.'"

Browning laughed, because that was exactly what he was planning to tell her. He needed to think of some other innocuous detail of the case.

"Well, I guess I can tell you who we are interviewing. We'll be talking to his students and colleagues," he said, knowing that most people would expect that regardless of whether the newspaper mentioned it or not.

Sarah groaned. "Mark, everyone figures that anyway. How about giving me some names?"

He shook his head. "Sorry. No way."

She sighed. She had heard first-hand that a female student reported to police that the professor was having trouble with one of his students. That detail, along with Mark's remark, would make for an interesting tidbit in her story. It wasn't much, but it was enough to satisfy her.

"Okay, you win," she relented, sliding off the desk. "I guess I have enough for today's deadline, but I'll be needing more for the next issue. I have to run now."

Browning stood and closed his office door, then took her in his arms and covered her mouth with his. He might be hard-headed when it came to dealing with the press, Sarah thought, but he sure was a great kisser.

Chapter Six

Sarah pulled her pickup into a parking spot on the street directly in front of the *Times* building, a vintage concrete block structure painted clay red with white shutters on the front windows. It was a block from Sapphire Lake, where Sarah often walked to spend the few minutes she managed to squeeze into her day for a bag lunch.

The morning had broken with a warm breeze off Lake Michigan, unusual for early spring. Sarah heard the voice of Martha Scott—the newspaper's receptionist, classified ad manager and town gossip—floating out the screen door as she stepped from her pickup.

"How's this for beautiful weather, honey? I'm leaving the door open and airing out the place!"

The door, framed in wood with a gingerbread design, closed with a bang behind Sarah. "Hi, Martha," she said, inhaling the welcome addition of fresh air in the winter-weary interior. "Is Mr. Jakes in yet?"

Vernon Jakes, the publisher, rarely made it to the office until late morning. If he wasn't attending chamber of commerce meetings or dealing with other business interests, he was indulging in another favorite activity—fishing.

"Oh, yes," Martha said, picking lint balls from her pink knit sweater. "He was here early and said you should go directly to his office when you get in. I'm guessing he wants to find out the scoop on the professor's murder last night. I can't believe you found the body!"

Sarah smiled to herself. Martha knew almost everyone in town and usually was one of the first to hear about breaking news. Her connections had often proven valuable to Sarah.

"What have you heard about it, Martha?"

It was the opening Martha had been waiting for. She raised her plump, sixty-six-year-old body from her chair and rubbed her hands together, walking over to Sarah and talking in a whisper.

"Well, my friend Alma has a grandson in the sheriff's department, and he was at the scene last night. He said the professor was viciously stabbed by a student who was mad at him for some reason. I mean, Professor Lichner was a cold fish, but he didn't deserve to be stabbed, for heaven's sake!"

Sarah's interest was piqued. "You knew the professor, Martha?"

Martha patted her dyed red hair, short and stiffly

permed into place. "Why, of course. I'm a member of the historical society, and he was our president. You cannot believe how many boring lectures he would give at our meetings, but we elected him to the position because he was so knowledgeable. Sometimes, his talks ran so long that we would practically starve waiting to have the coffee and doughnuts we'd serve after the meeting. He hardly ever stayed for the refreshments."

"Not too sociable, huh?"

Martha winked. "Well, not with us, but he was very sociable for a time with a certain library director."

Sarah was surprised. "You mean Beth Callison? The college's school board president?"

Martha put her finger to her mouth, shushing Sarah. "Don't say you got it from me, but they were dating for a few months until he dumped her. At least, that's what my friends at the library say. They think he was the one who broke it off because Beth Callison was dragging around for a few weeks acting like she'd lost her best friend. He was no prize, but I honestly don't know what he saw in her in the first place. She was kind of nasty, always looking down her nose at us when she'd attend a historical society function. But that's about all I know, dear."

Sarah patted her on the arm. "Thanks, Martha. Keep me posted if you hear anything else, okay?"

"Oh, I'll hear something else, honey. By the way, how's that gorgeous fiancé of yours? Are you two getting excited about the wedding? I've already marked that date on my calendar."

Sarah told her about the problem she was having

deciding on a veil, listening to all of Martha's suggestions that sounded like fashion advice from a 1950s bridal magazine. Talking to Martha always reminded her how much she missed her mother, back home in a suburb of Chicago. Sarah made a mental note to call her that night to discuss wedding plans and just to talk.

She headed into the newsroom and turned on her computer, checking for stories that her stringers, or part-time reporters, had filed the night before. Holly was her only full-time reporter. Together, the two of them handled the bulk of what was happening in Potter County. She had been begging Mr. Jakes to hire one more reporter, but the bottom line was more important to him than spreading the workload around more fairly.

She glanced at the stories, then at her watch, and decided she had a few minutes to see Mr. Jakes before editing the articles and writing her own. Straightening the bottom of her black cotton blouse over her light grey skirt, she walked up the one flight of creaky wooden stairs to her publisher's office.

He was bent over a car dealership ad due to run in tomorrow's issue. It was for an important advertiser and he wanted to make sure it was free of mistakes.

"Morning, Mr. Jakes," she said, knocking on the open door.

A short man who always wore his trousers belted high on his thin waist, Jakes stood. He *always* stood when a woman entered the room, a gesture that Sarah admired for its gentility, but one that made her feel awkward.

"Good morning, Sarah. Have a seat. There are a few things I need to discuss with you."

His manner was serious, and Sarah prepared herself for a problem.

"I received this in yesterday's mail and just opened it this morning," he said, reaching for an envelope on his desk. "It concerns me, because I thought we had put this behind us. But, I guess it's back again."

He opened the envelope and withdrew a piece of paper, handing it to Sarah. It was the same letter that someone had left at her cottage.

"I got this, too, Mr. Jakes," she said, recounting the events of the night before. "I discussed it with Mark, and we decided it could be someone starting some political shenanigans to cause him problems."

Jakes wrinkled his brow. "Politics? Already? The sheriff's race is more than three years away and no one has indicated an interest in running against Browning. Personally, I think it's a reader, and that worries me. How many of our readers feel this way, I wonder? If we lose readers, we lose advertisers."

She read it again, biting her lip. "If it's a reader who thinks we'll lose our objectivity because of my relationship with Mark, then all I can do to correct that misperception is to continue reporting the news as I always have. Certainly, Mr. Jakes, if other readers felt like this, we would hear about it."

Jakes drummed his pen on his desk, frowning. "I *do* have several conversations with readers during the course of my day, and no one has complained about your reporting on sheriff's department activities. In fact, several members of the business community have chuckled about how tough you seem to be on your own fiancé."

She dropped the letter on his desk. "Honestly, I sometimes think I'm *too* tough on Mark. Kind of over-compensating, I guess. But I'll make sure that I continue to be as aggressive with police news as I am with other stories. We should expect things like this from time to time, though."

He leaned back in his leather swivel chair, satisfied that the letter was not as serious as he first thought. "Speaking of police news, what's the story with last night's murder? Martha said you found the body."

Sarah grinned. "She probably gave you as much information as I have." She provided him with every-thing she knew. "Actually, Martha told me a few things that I want to check on for the next issue."

"Good," Jakes said, lightly pounding his fist on his desk. "Don't let that boyfriend of yours put a muzzle on you. Everyone at the chamber of commerce meeting last night was concerned. This is the second murder in a year in Potter County, and we sure don't need such things scaring the tourists away. We need to put pres-sure on the sheriff to get this thing solved."

Sarah had an hour before deadline. She hurried back to her desk, rapidly editing the stringers' stories and sending them to the print shop. Then she worked on her own front page story, efficiently relaying the facts of the murder in a concise but compelling style. She led her article with the meager details on the progress of the investigation because, by the time readers received her twice-weekly paper the next day, most would already know that the professor had been murdered.

Holly had arrived soon after Sarah began writing, tapping on her own keyboard as she wrote the story on the interrupted school board meeting. Once both stories were filed, Sarah finally poured herself the cup of morning coffee she hadn't had time to get earlier.

"So, who do they think killed him?" Holly asked as Sarah settled back at her desk. "I saw Mark and Thompson hanging around the school board meeting after it ended. Who did they talk to?"

"Hmm," Sarah mumbled through a mouthful of coffee, swallowing quickly as that information sunk in. "I'm guessing they found out the same thing I did— that Lichner and Beth Callison had been seeing each other."

Holly's eyes opened wide. "Really? So maybe she knows something? Oh, man, this could get really interesting! Ooo, if I'd known that, I would have checked out her clothing for blood or something!"

Sarah laughed, enjoying the veteran reporter's continuing fascination with intriguing news stories. Holly had passed her love of journalism and interest in politics on to her two children, both of whom were studying those subjects at the state university.

"I think Mark would have noticed the blood, but knowing him, he wouldn't say a word to me," Sarah said. "I also heard that the professor was having problems with one of his students. I plan on checking out both of these leads."

"Does Mark know that?"

Sarah shook her head. "Mark doesn't need to know about what I'm doing until I learn something I might need to talk to him about. That's the way we have to operate or we'd drive each other crazy."

She flipped back through a few pages in her notebook, looking for a name she had written down the night before. She found it. Heather Bergen. The deputy had announced it when he got in trouble with Mark.

Grabbing the phone book from a bottom drawer, Sarah flipped to the Bs and ran her finger down the list until she reached Bergen. There were four names listed, with three Bergens living in Hillcrest. She hoped one of the numbers belonged to Heather. It wouldn't take too long to find out.

Her first call was answered by an elderly man who told her she had the wrong number. She hit the jackpot on her second try.

"Just a minute, please," a melodic female voice said when she asked to speak to Heather. Sarah recognized the voice of the young woman who soon came on the line. It was the same voice she had briefly overheard when Mark talked to her in the hallway of the social sciences building, before he led Heather away from prying ears.

"Heather? My name is Sarah Carpenter, and I'm editor of the *Potter County Times*. Do you have a minute to talk to me?" she asked politely.

There was a moment of silence on the other end, long enough for Sarah to wonder if Heather had hung up.

"Um . . . why?" Heather said quietly.

"Well, I'm writing a story on Professor Lichner's murder and I understand you have some pertinent information regarding a student the professor was having trouble with. I saw you at the scene and then again this morning at the sheriff's department."

"Uh huh. So?"

Sarah didn't want to scare her off. "I know of several people the police need to talk to, and I want to make sure I have the correct name of the student. Can you tell me what it is?"

Heather sniffed. "Certainly not. I'm working with the sheriff on this case and I know that Mark would not want me to talk to a reporter."

Mark? Where does she get off calling my Mark, Mark?

"You're working with the police? What are you doing for them?"

Heather hesitated again before answering. "I have some training in criminal investigation," she said with pride, "plus I knew the victim and I know one of the suspects. I'm sure Mark values my assistance."

If she uses his first name one more time, I'm calling her on it.

"So, you're saying that the police consider this student to be a suspect?" Sarah asked, telling herself to take all information from this young flirt with a grain of salt.

"Like I said, I'm not going to talk to you about the investigation."

Sarah persisted and played into Heather's ego. "Okay, I understand your need as an investigator to keep details secret. Just for my information—not for print—do you consider this student to be the prime suspect?"

Heather sighed. "It's possible that Matt had nothing to do with it, but we'll find out, that's for sure."

Matt! Sarah scribbled the name in her notebook.

"Well, thanks for your time, Heather. Maybe I'll give you another call in case you learn something you can tell me."

Heather laughed. "Oh, I doubt I'll be able to disclose anything to you. You should just talk to the sheriff. You know him quite well, don't you?"

Sarah wrinkled her brow, wondering what that was supposed to mean. "Ah . . . kind of. Thanks again."

Holly was looking at Sarah. "Your face is all flushed. Someone make you mad?"

Sarah pointed at the phone. "This girl is freaky. She's this perky blond student who latched on to Mark last night, claiming to have information about another student who was giving Lichner problems. She won't talk to me because she says she's working with Mark on the case and—get this—she calls him Mark!"

"I see. Jealousy rearing its ugly head," Holly joked.

"No, I just think she's a bit deluded. I bet Mark thinks the same thing."

"Or not." Holly smiled. "She might really have some important information, Sarah, and she might have a crush on your beloved, but I don't think you need to worry about Mark."

Sarah leaned back in her chair, tapping her lip with an index finger. "Am I really the jealous type?"

Holly answered without skipping a beat. "Yeah, but in a good way. Not in a nutty, *Fatal Attraction* way. I'll let you know if you start acting crazy." She turned back to the story she was working on.

Sarah stared at her notes. If Heather truly was working with Mark on the case, it would indicate that Matt what's-his-name was, indeed, a bonafide suspect. This would be real news for her next story, although she would not print his name if she learned it. The newspaper's policy was to print the names only of people who had been charged with a crime, not those merely suspected of one. Doing otherwise could get them in legal trouble.

She dialed Mark's office number and he immediately picked up.

"You're calling back already? You barely left here!"

She tried to sound nonchalant. "Just checking on something with you. I happened to talk to Heather Bergen, that student who approached you with information last night, and she told me she's working with you on the case."

Browning exhaled a muffled expletive. "How . . . where did you talk to her?"

It wasn't the amused reaction that Sarah expected. "I had her name and I called her. Is it true?"

He ignored the question. "What else did she tell you?"

Sarah raised an eyebrow. "How about answering my question first?"

Browning sighed. "No, she's not working on the case with us. She gave us some information that may or may not be helpful, that's all. I think she's just kind of a—how should I say this—law enforcement groupie."

"Seems more like a Mark Browning groupie to me. She talked like you two are best friends." Sarah winced after speaking. Her jealous side was showing. "Anyway, she didn't say much except she indicated that you consider this certain student to be a suspect."

"She's wrong. We haven't gotten nearly far enough to call anyone a suspect. And, hon, I'm keeping this kid at arm's length. Don't put any credence in anything she tells you. She's a little mesmerized with all of this, and it will pass."

Sarah felt a bit silly. "Guess I don't like it when blond bombshells are lusting after my man, even ones young enough to be your daughter."

"Hey, you're the only bombshell I look at," he assured her. "Speaking of that, how about dinner tonight? I missed our ice cream date last night."

They agreed to meet at The Antler restaurant after

work for one of the eatery's famous cheeseburgers. But before then, Sarah had some work cut out for her.

She needed to talk to another person whose name Martha had supplied—Beth Callison.

Chapter Seven

Matt Baker wasn't a stranger to the sheriff's department. As a juvenile, he had been arrested two times for residential burglary and once for selling marijuana to students at his high school. Because of his young age at the time, he had received what amounted to slaps on the wrist from the court system. Baker was now twenty years old, and police believed he had been involved in several other burglaries and thefts in the county. They just couldn't prove it.

Thompson knew Baker worked mornings at his father's marina in Franklin, a nearby Lake Michigan beach town. He was in charge of the place until Baker Sr. arrived around noon.

"Like the Bergen girl said, the old man is grooming the kid to take over the business some day," Thompson told Browning as they pulled into the marina parking lot. They wanted to interview Baker without a parent around. Usually, kids were extra talkative if they wanted to prevent the cops from contacting their parents.

The boating season hadn't quite begun, and most of the slips in the marina were still empty. Gulls screamed overhead as the men stepped out of Browning's unmarked car. The birds dove toward the parking lot to retrieve scraps of hamburger buns and French fries discarded by early season tourists, oblivious to the humans walking no more than a foot away from them.

"Lousy birds," Thompson muttered. "They already messed up your windshield."

The men entered the small, vinyl-sided building at the edge of the lot near the marina's numerous docks. They spotted Matt Baker in an office behind the main lobby and no one met them at the front counter. They were glad about that—they didn't need a nosy employee notifying the father that the police were talking to his son.

Baker looked up when Browning cleared his throat. He narrowed his eyes when he recognized Thompson, slamming his pencil on his desk.

"Well, surprise, surprise," Baker said sarcastically. Strings from the frayed bottoms of his low-slung jeans dragged across the floor as he walked to the counter. Despite a slender physique, Baker obviously had worked at developing taut muscles, apparent under a black T-shirt bearing the name of a famous rap group. His hair hung almost to his eyes and over his ears in the style popular among his contemporaries. Small features and smooth skin made him look younger than his twenty years.

"I wondered how long it would be before you tried to pin Lichner's murder on me," he said.

"How did you find out about it so quickly, Matt?" Thompson asked him.

"Are you kidding? I had three or four phone calls from people in my class last night. This town ain't that big, Detective."

He glanced at Browning, then at the badge on his belt.

"Oh, yeah," Thompson said. "This is Sheriff Browning. He works in that big office you pass in the hallway whenever we bring you in to the department for causing more trouble."

Baker, used to Thompson's putdowns, ignored the reference to his past. "Wow," he snickered. "You're sending the big guns after me now, huh?"

Browning motioned to the office. "C'mon, Matt. How about we sit down in there and clear this up? We need to talk to you just like we've been talking to everyone else who knew the professor."

Baker laughed. "Yeah, right," he said as he headed into the room. "I don't care. I really ain't got nothing to tell you."

Baker and Thompson sat in the two chairs in the office and Browning remained standing, his arms folded.

"First of all, Matt, who called you last night about the murder? Friends?" Browning asked.

Baker shrugged. "I hang out with a couple of them every now and then—Adam Knowles and Andy . . . I don't know his last name. We're not really that tight, you know? They got a call from a girl in our class, and they just wanted to see if I'd heard the same thing."

He sat slouched in the chair, both feet on the floor and knees rapidly knocking together. Thompson leaned forward and put a steadying hand on one of his legs, stopping the movement.

"Nervous, Matt?" he asked.

Baker gave him a sour look and crossed one leg over the other.

"Who's the girl in your class who called them?" Browning asked.

"Heather Bergen. She called me too. I went to high school with her but I don't know her too good. I have no idea why she called me, but I guess she was calling everybody in class."

Browning looked at Thompson, who had raised his eyes to the ceiling in frustration. He was losing patience with their helpful schoolgirl.

"She ask you any questions?" Thompson said in disgust.

Baker looked confused. "Why the hell would she ask me questions? She was just all excited about it—she's into this crime stuff—and wanted to gossip about it. We didn't talk much. I just said, 'Wow, no kidding,' and hung up. I couldn't believe it happened."

"When did she call you?" Browning asked.

Baker leaned back, smoothing back his hair with both hands. "I'd say around nine-thirty or ten o'clock. Yeah, that's right, because the news came on shortly after I talked to her, and my dad was watching it. He told me it was on the news."

Browning sat on the edge of the desk, close to Baker. "Matt, tell us what you did last night from, say, five o'clock until you got the phone call from Miss Bergen."

Baker rolled his eyes and threw up his hands. "I knew it! You're not just talking to people who knew Lichner—you think I might have done it! Why would you think that?"

Thompson stopped chewing on a toothpick and removed it from his mouth, twirling it between two fingers. Keeping his mouth and hands constantly active had become incessant after quitting smoking a few months earlier.

"Just answer the question, kid. We're not accusing you of anything," he said roughly.

Face flushed and legs starting to bounce again, Baker angrily recounted his day. "I had Lichner's class from five o'clock until six-fifteen. Then, I stopped at the McDonald's drive-in in Hillcrest and got some food. I drove over to Sleeping Bear Beach and ate my food there. Then I went home."

"What time did you get home?" Thompson asked.

Baker looked at the floor, rubbing a scuff mark with the toe of his sneakers. "I don't know . . . maybe a little after eight o'clock."

Browning scratched his cheek. "You're telling us it

took you two hours to get some food and eat it at the beach? That beach is only ten minutes from Hillcrest."

Baker's face was flushed. "I like to sit at the beach, okay? I finished my food and hung around for a while before I went home."

Browning stood up and looked out the window. "You're failing Lichner's class, right, Matt? And that test you took yesterday probably didn't help, did it? Chances to get that money your dad promised you if you graduate this year are looking pretty slim, aren't they?"

Baker gripped the sides of his chair. "How did you know about the money?" He stood and began to pace the room, tight-lipped and breathing heavily. "You know," he said, stopping and pointing at Browning, "you should check out what Lichner's been involved in. Where'd he get all his money? That jerk had wads of cash lying all over his house! Maybe *that's* what got him killed!"

Hands in his pockets, Browning calmly turned away from the window and looked at Baker.

"And when did you see cash in his house, Matt?" he asked.

Baker exhaled and sat down, putting his elbows on his knees and holding his head in his hands. The men let him take his time to answer.

"Okay, I'll tell you this if you promise I won't get in trouble. It was no big deal," he said, a look of desperation on his face.

Browning nodded. "Agreed. What'd you do?"

He hung his head again and directed his explanation at the floor. "So, like, three or four months ago, Lichner starts coming to class with these expensive suits and, like, a Rolex watch and stuff. Then I see him after class getting in a new BMW, so I'm thinking, hey, this dude must have more bucks than a normal community college teacher."

Browning sat back down on the edge of the desk. "So, you decide to check out his house, right?"

Baker shrugged. "Well, yeah. I mean, I didn't break in or nothing. I knocked on the door, figuring that if he was there, I'd give some excuse about wanting to talk to him about my grade. But he didn't answer, so I tried the door. It was open."

Thompson interrupted. "And you saw no reason not to go inside and make yourself at home."

Baker shot the detective a disdainful look. "Fool leaves his door open, he's asking for it. Anyway, I see two piles of cash right away. One's sitting on the kitchen table, and one's on his desk in his den. I grabbed them and ran. I swear, he had more than three thousand dollars sitting out in the open like that."

Thompson snorted. "Kid, when are ya gonna learn? One day, you're gonna land in jail and they'll be throwing away the key."

Baker stuck to his story during the remainder of the interview, repeating the details of his activities when asked. Browning warned him not to leave the area, assuring him that he'd be questioned again soon.

"So, what do you make of his story?" Thompson asked as they headed back to the department.

Browning turned off the police scanner in the car, its scratchy broadcasts making it difficult to carry on a conversation. "We've got two main things to check out, Charlie. Number one—Matt's lack of an alibi for last night. Number two—Lichner's sudden wealth, if Matt is telling the truth. Don't know why he'd jeopardize his own hide like that to throw us off track, though. His info could be legit."

Thompson agreed. "And what's interesting is that Lichner never reported the theft to us. I'll check on that, but I read all the daily reports and I'm sure I'd remember that one. Could be he didn't want us to know about the cash in his house."

Browning tapped the steering wheel with his finger, thinking. "I want to talk to Beth Callison again, see if she knew anything about his finances." Briefly looking at Thompson, he added, "We also need to check on her alibi for last night. And we need to do a search of Lichner's home. If he had stacks of money lying around, let's see what other interesting things we might find."

The detective rolled down his window and spit out a sunflower seed. "And do me a favor? Tell your little girlfriend—and I don't mean Sarah—to keep her nose out of our business. That kid is starting to annoy me."

Browning grinned and nodded. "Will do, Charlie. I'll

politely tell her to butt out. She's starting to annoy someone else, too . . . my *real* girlfriend."

Sarah finished the last bite of her turkey sandwich and crumpled her paper lunch bag into a ball, tossing it in the garbage can next to the Sapphire Lake Park bench she was sitting on. Grabbing her bottle of water, she began a slow walk back to the office, inspecting the park's gardens filled with tulips nearly ready to burst open.

She needed to fetch her purse and keys from her desk before heading to the Hillcrest Public Library for an interview with Beth Callison. In a morning phone call, the school board president and library director had first refused Sarah's request to talk.

"It's just too difficult to talk about him right now," she had said.

But Sarah reminded her of Lichner's status in the community—as a professor and as president of the historical society. "I would like our readers to know about his accomplishments and how much he did for the community," Sarah urged. "I've been told you knew him well and could provide some information for my next article on him, which will focus more on his life than his death."

It wasn't a completely honest description of the next story, but Sarah only felt slightly guilty about that. And it worked. Callison reluctantly agreed to meet with her after lunch.

Before leaving the office, Sarah questioned Holly about the controversy at last night's board meeting.

Any information concerning Callison would be helpful in her interview.

"I know there's been a problem with the school spending a lot of money on a project that doesn't look completed, and some taxpayers are upset," she said. "Any more you can tell me other than what was in the story you wrote this morning?"

Holly shook her head. "No, that's the problem. The board has been unable to explain why it apparently under-budgeted for the renovations on the historic buildings. Some people are blaming the contractors of charging more than they bid and others say the school's finances were mishandled. In any case, the board is proposing to increase taxes to help cover the extra money needed to finish the job—not a popular move. Callison pretty much keeps her mouth shut. This is a hot potato she doesn't want to touch in public."

Sarah kept the information in the back of her mind as she drove to the library, knowing the main topic of conversation with Callison would be about the murder. She had spoken to her once before, when the library dedicated its new building two years before. It had moved from almost a small storefront operation to a state-of-the-art facility, with self-checkout kiosks for patrons and even a small coffee shop inside.

A woman at the circulation desk led her to Callison's office, a sunny space with expansive windows and a healthy ficus tree in the corner of the room. Callison, dressed in a black pants suit, rose to shake her hand.

"I don't know if I can help you much," she told Sarah. "Philip was a good teacher and a wonderful asset to the historical society, but that's about all I can tell you concerning his public life."

Sarah started off slowly, avoiding the topic of their personal relationship so she wouldn't immediately alienate Callison.

"In what ways do you think Professor Lichner most helped his community?" she asked.

Callison rested her chin on her hands, dark circles prominent under her eyes. She looked to Sarah as if sleep had been difficult to come by lately.

"Well, obviously he was an asset to our youth. The knowledge he passed on to them was invaluable, of course. He was a tough teacher, but his students probably learned more because of that. I know some of his students couldn't adjust to his style, though."

Sarah wondered if she should ask about any specific student who was having trouble with Lichner, then decided to wait. She jotted a few notes. "And his work in the historical society—what achievements could be attributed to him?"

Callison became animated. "I was very proud of the work he did on the college's behalf through his involvement with the historical society. He was quite familiar with the significance of some of our buildings, which were erected in the 1800s. Because of his research and the connections he established through the society, we were awarded a grant from the National Historic Preservation Foundation. It was very helpful in funding our current renovation efforts."

Sarah paused as she wrote, deciding to broach the subject of the budget controversy. "That must have been a godsend considering the budget problems caused by the project, I would guess."

Callison sighed. "Yes, it certainly didn't hurt. We are currently investigating our finances to determine what caused the discrepancies, and our project manager, Tom Barrett, is working on it too. That's all I can tell you at the moment."

Sarah looked up from her notebook. Callison's mouth was firmly set and she had folded her arms in front of her. It was definitely not a topic she wanted to discuss with a newspaper editor. So, Sarah changed the subject.

"A member of the historical society told me that you and the professor were rather close for a while, so this must have been quite a shock for you," she said, trying to tiptoe into a discussion about the murder.

Callison was not pleased. "Yes, it was extremely upsetting to me, and I wish people would not find it necessary to announce my personal business around town. We were friends, that's all."

Sarah put down her pen. Often, a person would open up if the reporter appeared not to be recording every word.

"I know what you mean. Everyone starts to gossip when something like this happens and it's hard to know what to believe. I was told that it was difficult for you when the professor decided to . . . well . . . end your relationship. Now, *this* happens. It's crazy what people think."

Sarah's inference was clear, as much as she tried to blame the idea on town gossip. It infuriated Callison.

"I should have known when you called that you had ulterior motives," she said bitterly. "I'd like you to leave right now."

Sarah didn't move. "Have the police questioned you about the murder?"

Callison simply stood and walked to the door, holding it open. Sarah noted the trembling hand that gripped the edge of the door as she walked past her.

Tossing her notebook on the car seat and sliding behind the wheel, Sarah knew she probably wouldn't be welcomed back for another interview. Callison's heated reaction to the question about her relationship with Lichner was understandable and didn't reveal any new information, Sarah decided.

But, she thought, the connection between Lichner's work at the historical society and the controversial renovation project at the college might prove to be interesting.

Chapter Eight

Browning told Thompson to round up a couple of deputies to help them scour Lichner's home for clues. The victim was the sole owner and occupant of the home, so a search warrant was not necessary.

But first, he needed to make a phone call. He found Heather Bergen's cell phone number in the notes he'd taken when talking to her at the murder scene, never expecting he'd have to use it. She answered in a breathless voice after several rings.

"Heather? It's Sheriff Browning. I'm hoping I'm not interrupting something important."

"Not at all!" She almost squealed in delight at hearing his voice. "I'm just walking to a class. Do you need me to do something in the case?"

He wanted to let her down easy. "Heather, your enthusiasm about police work is really admirable, and I hope you continue to pursue it in your studies," he said gently. "But I've been told you contacted Matt Baker regarding this case, and we really would prefer that you not become as involved as you have been. It really could hurt our investigation."

He could hear a petulant sigh on the other end. "All I did was let Matt know what happened. There's no harm in that, is there? And maybe he would have said something incriminating. You wouldn't be complaining about me if that happened!"

A firmer approach was necessary. "Heather, we don't need your help. I appreciate the offer, but no thanks. It's that plain and simple. If we have any more questions, we'll contact you."

She hung up on him. He was glad she got the message.

He found Thompson in the department's lunchroom, buying a pack of gum from one of the vending machines, and the two drove to Philip Lichner's house in Hillcrest. Befitting an historian, it was a classically turreted Victorian elaborately painted in two shades of green, deep red and cream. The porch alone, with intricate trim work on numerous balusters, must have taken days to paint.

Deputies had found Lichner's house and car keys on his office desk at the college. They later discovered that the house had been left open the night before, then locked it to keep out the curious. Browning remembered this when Matt Baker described an open door the day he stole the money. The professor must have been a trusting sort, Browning decided.

Two deputies entered the home with Browning and Thompson.

"Just look for anything interesting, guys. Keep your gloves on and handle things carefully. Check out garbage cans, clothes, everything," he advised.

They did a quick check of every room, looking for an item that might immediately grab their attention. Nothing did—everything appeared normal, and it was apparent that Lichner was a tidy housekeeper.

"Charlie, let's you and me take a look in his desk. That's where I'd put *my* personal stuff. We'll also bring his computer back to the department for Barone to go over." Then Browning turned to the deputies. "You guys start picking over the rest of his stuff."

Two desk drawers were filled with common office supplies. The bottom drawer, much deeper than the others, contained a filing system with neatly organized documents. Browning flipped through the labeled topics, including household necessities, bill payments and classroom paperwork. He withdrew the file folders containing Lichner's personal financial information. It might be helpful in determining whether he did, indeed, suddenly become a wealthy man.

One file sat on top of the desk, labeled Grant Application. Browning withdrew the papers and studied them.

"Whatcha got?" Thompson asked while paging through the other files.

"Hmm. Looks like the college applied for some kind of historic preservation grant," he said, then picked up another piece of paper and read it. "Whew! We're not talking small change here. Take a look at this, Charlie."

Thompson read it out loud. "The National Historic Preservation Foundation is pleased to inform you that Hillcrest College has been selected to receive the foundation's annual five-hundred-thousand-dollar grant in its effort to maintain and enhance the landmarks from our country's past."

He looked up at Browning. "And that school has budget problems? They must have a bunch of numbskulls running the place if they couldn't put half a mil to good use."

Browning rubbed his chin. "Beth Callison and her school board cohorts are running the place, Charlie. Very interesting. We'll take this file with us, too, obviously."

They heard a deputy shout from a room upstairs.

"Got something for you to look at, Sheriff!" he called.

Browning took the stairs two at a time. Thompson followed slowly behind, huffing and puffing.

"In here, Sheriff," the deputy said from a room off the top of the stairway. With its ornate four-poster bed and huge elegant armoire, Browning guessed it was Lichner's master bedroom.

The deputy was near the closet, one finger holding a hanger that carried a tan, belted raincoat.

"Wanted you to see this before I bag it," the deputy said, smiling. "Look at the pocket area."

Browning and Thompson both crouched and

peered at the pocket. The outer material and the pocket flap were smeared with what appeared to be dried blood.

"Well, I'll be damned," Thompson said quietly.

"Look in the pocket," the deputy said. "There's more in there."

Browning lifted the flap and held the pocket open with two gloved hands. Inside was more of the brownish stain, wiped along both sides of the pocket's enclosure.

"How the hell did this get back here if it was at the murder scene?" Browning wondered.

Thompson stood slowly, hiking up his pants when he rose. "Maybe it wasn't there. Maybe it's blood from something else."

"Fold it carefully and bag it. We'll get it to Barone to type the blood, check for fibers, hair . . . maybe even prints if he can lift some. We don't even know if this belongs to Lichner. But if it's the killer's, why would he plant it in Lichner's closet?"

Thompson tapped his foot on the floor. "I'm guessing it's Lichner's. The killer might have worn it, maybe to conceal the weapon, and didn't notice the blood. He might have figured the best way to get rid of the raincoat would be to put it back in Lichner's closet."

Browning slowly nodded. "It was raining last night. It's possible Lichner had this coat at school. If he leaves his office unlocked like he leaves his house open, anyone could have found it and put it on. Then, they might have thought it too risky—"

"—to return it to his office," Thompson finished. "The perp wanted to hightail it out of that school building as quickly as possible, then found himself strapped with this raincoat."

It made sense to Browning. "But, what did he do with the weapon and where did he get it? Did he walk into the building carrying a seven-inch knife for all to see? Deputy, have you guys checked everything? Drawers, garbage, in the toilet tanks . . . you know what I mean."

The deputy assured him that the house had been scoured. "And, Sheriff, you can hide a seven-inch knife in a waistband under your shirt, easy. He might have gone to Lichner's office first, seen this coat and figured it would work better. You can lift a knife from a pocket quicker than fumbling under a shirt for it."

All in all, the search party came away with eight paper bags filled with documents, personal items, clothing—and the prized raincoat.

Browning and Thompson were silent on the way back to the department, except for Thompson's periodic humming of "Whistle While You Work." Upon his fourth rendition, Browning told him to change his tune.

"You know what I was thinking, boss?" he offered instead. "Getting rid of the raincoat might not have been the bad guy's reason for going to Lichner's house after the murder. There might have been another purpose."

"And what would that be, Charlie?"

Thompson looked over at Browning with a raised eyebrow.

"He might've been lookin' for more piles of cash."

Browning slowed the unmarked car as it neared the Hillcrest Public Library, then made a quick turn into the parking lot.

"Need some reading material?" Thompson asked dryly.

"Let's pay a visit to Beth Callison. I have a couple of questions for her."

A circulation desk librarian notified Callison that two police officers were there to speak with her. She stepped outside her office and motioned for them to come inside, prompting the nearby staff to exchange curious looks.

Callison exhaled loudly as she walked toward her desk, offering the men a seat.

"It's been a difficult day, and this isn't making it any easier," she complained. "Why are you here?"

Browning leaned forward. "We'll just get to the point. As someone who was close to Philip Lichner, you need to tell us where you were in the hours before his death—say, from five o'clock yesterday until after the board meeting."

She slapped her palms on the desk. "This is very insulting. I am director of the library and president of the community college's school board. How can you possibly justify asking me such a question?"

Browning folded his hands in his lap and sat back in

the chair. "We don't *need* to justify it, ma'am, and because of the positions you hold, you should understand better than most that we need to collect as much information as possible to solve this case for the community."

His comment appealed enough to her public service mindset that she gave an immediate but disgruntled answer. "I worked here at the library until six o'clock. I decided to return to my condo for a quick bite to eat before going to the college for our meeting. After eating a sandwich at home, I lied on the couch to rest my eyes for a moment because it had been a hectic day. It wasn't like me, but I fell asleep and didn't wake up until seven-fifteen. I barely made it back in time for our seven-thirty meeting."

"Did anyone see you between the time you left the library and arrived at the board meeting?" Browning asked.

She twirled a ring on her right hand. "No. No one saw me at my home and I went directly into the boardroom after parking my car at the college. Does that make me a murderer?" she asked with sarcasm.

Browning noted the lack of an alibi and moved on to another question. "Professor Lichner apparently acquired a substantial amount of money recently and was able to buy an expensive car and other items. What do you know about this?"

She appeared befuddled at first and then suddenly amused. "Oh, you mean the BMW? That was just a gift from his father, whom I guess is quite well off. Philip said it was a present for his fortieth birthday a few months ago. Trust me. Philip was *not* a wealthy man."

Thompson's tongue skillfully moved his toothpick to one side of his mouth so he could speak. "It's not just the car, Ms. Callison. We hear there'd been expensive suits, jewelry . . . lots of cash."

She pressed a finger to her temple and looked down at her lap. "Well, I wouldn't know about that. As I said, we hadn't been dating lately."

She continued to deny knowledge of Lichner's finances, then grew agitated when Browning questioned her about the historic preservation grant given to the college.

"What in the world does that have to do with Philip's murder? That money was acquired for the college through his hard work and dedication, it was well deserved and it is being put to proper use!"

Browning tapped his thumbs together. "It is difficult to understand how the college could encounter such serious budget problems with the renovation project if you had an extra five-hundred-thousand dollars to help fund it," he said bluntly.

She threw up her hands. "Oh, yes, I agree!" she spat out. "Maybe you should talk to our finance director, Tom Barrett. So far, he's been unable to answer that question for our school board as well! And now, I think it is time for you to leave," she stated flatly, her mouth twitching as she waited for them to exit the room.

"So, what do you think about her, Charlie?" Browning asked as they drove to the department.

"Let's see. No alibi, boyfriend dumped her, kind of an angry sort."

"Do we put her on the list?"

Thompson pulled a box of Raisinets from his pocket and shook about a dozen into his mouth.

"Yeah," he mumbled through a mouthful of chocolate. "Put her on the list."

After sorting through the collected evidence, giving Barone what he needed to analyze and stacking the rest in his office, Browning rushed home to get changed for his dinner date with Sarah.

He couldn't wait to move out of his apartment after marrying Sarah. He barely spent any time there, using it mostly as a place to sleep, so it had remained much the same as the day he moved in—sparsely filled with cheap furniture, barren walls and none of the personal touches that made Sarah's cottage so inviting. Some days, when the art store on the first floor beneath him was busy, the noise became bothersome. And the view from his windows, which looked over Hillcrest's main street, could never compare to Lake Michigan.

It had turned a bit chilly later in the afternoon, so Browning changed into a pair of tan corduroys and a forest-green sweater. He checked himself out in the mirror. His dark five o'clock shadow was in full bloom, and he briefly considered a quick shave. Glancing at his watch, he decided against it. Anyway, Sarah always told him she thought the stubble made him look mysterious and sexy, although he never believed that.

Sarah needed only to cross the street from her office to reach The Antler, so they decided to meet there. He saw her stepping on to the curb in front of the restaurant just as he pulled into a parking spot on the street, and she smiled and waved. He loved looking at her as the breeze lifted her dark brown hair off her pretty face and molded her outfit to her slender curves.

"Hi, beautiful," he said gently as they kissed hello. "You look great."

Never able to take a compliment well, Sarah shooed him with a wave of her hand. "I probably look like something the cat dragged in with these work clothes. Plus, my hair's all straggly because I didn't have time to wash it this morning, and I—"

He quieted her with another hard kiss on the mouth. "Shush! You're beautiful!"

She lowered her head, embarrassed. "You are too," she whispered.

"No, I'm *handsome,*" he corrected her with a laugh.

The hostess smiled at their conversation as she led them to a table. It was in a corner where they had a full view of the room, adorned with varying sizes of deer antlers on the walls and laden with emptied peanut shells on the floor.

They both ordered cheeseburgers. None could compare to those served at The Antler. Cooked to perfection and seasoned with ingredients that the owner kept a secret, the burger was huge but rarely went unfinished. Between delicious bites, Sarah and Mark talked about the wedding.

"I'm kind of nervous about meeting your parents," she told him. They lived in New York and Browning was their only child. His father was a lawyer, and both parents had been disappointed when Mark chose not to follow in those footsteps. Although Browning eventually earned a master's degree in criminal justice, their continued disillusionment with his career choice caused a rift between them that hadn't yet been bridged. They had declined numerous invitations to travel to Michigan and meet Sarah. Browning had been too busy in his new job to take a trip to New York.

He put his hand over hers and squeezed it. "It'll be okay," he promised her. "And if you don't like them, we can just hang out with your family."

Sarah laughed. Her mother, two brothers and sister had welcomed Mark into the family with open arms. Hailing from three different states—Illinois, Indiana and across the country in Rhode Island—she couldn't see them and her extended family as often as she liked. She was looking forward to seeing them all very soon—and knew she'd miss her dad, who had died of cancer several years before.

Much to Browning's relief, their conversation hadn't touched on the murder—yet.

"I have to ask you something," Sarah began, prompting him to close his eyes and feign an anguished look. "Do you consider Beth Callison a suspect?"

His eyes popped open. "How do you know about Beth Callison?"

She shook her head. "That's not important. I just

need to know if she's someone who's on your list along with that Matt kid."

"What list? And who's Matt?" Browning asked in as puzzled a manner as he could muster.

She tapped her fork on the table, impatient. "You know what I'm talking about."

Browning grew more serious. "You know I can't discuss who we've been talking to. I just can't answer your questions, but I'd like to know who *you've* been talking to. Did Beth Callison contact you?"

She put down her fork and shrugged, holding up her hands. "Hey, I'm not going to divulge my information, either. But, I know you've talked to Matt and to Beth Callison, so I want to know if both are suspects."

He frowned. "Did Heather Bergen tell you we talked to Matt Baker? That still doesn't mean he's a suspect. And I assume your reporter at the school board meeting saw us talking to Beth Callison. Same goes for her. We're not ready to call anyone a suspect."

His comment confirmed that these two had been interviewed. Sarah would not use their names in her next story, but she could allude to the types of people police were looking at.

"And don't report that!" Browning added as he wagged a finger at her.

Ending their dinner on an adversarial note put a slight damper on the nice night they'd been having. Browning walked Sarah to her car and gave her a light kiss, promising to call her before turning in for the night.

"I don't like it when we're at cross purposes like this," he lamented. "But, I guess we better get used to it."

She nodded, putting her hands on each side of his face and kissing him again, this time long and deep. She knew they had to work hard at not letting their jobs come between them.

He smiled wanly and stepped back from the car. A look of alarm swept across his face as he glanced at her front tires. She looked at them and gasped.

"I've got two flats!" she said, then looked at them closer with narrowed eyes. "Have my tires been slashed?"

Browning crouched by one wheel, rubbing his finger over several gashes on its side. "Yeah, someone used something sharp on them, like a knife."

He stood and combed his fingers through his hair. "I'll call a tow and give you a ride home. Some kid must have been out slashing tires. I wonder if he got anyone else."

He looked at the cars parked near Sarah, all with fully inflated tires. Then, he looked across the street at his squad car. Its two front tires were both flat.

"Damn," he breathed, trotting over to his car. Both tires also had long gashes.

He turned and looked at Sarah. She looked back at him with worried eyes.

Someone had damaged their cars and hadn't touched any others.

Chapter Nine

Browning had the luxury of contacting an on-call auto repair service under contract to the sheriff's department. Help arrived within a few minutes. Sarah, on the other hand, needed to call a tow. Her pickup would sit in a tire shop's parking lot overnight.

The mechanic changing Browning's tires asked nothing when the sheriff retrieved a pair of latex evidence gloves from the trunk of his car and told him to put them on before touching the wheels. It was Sarah who peppered him with questions.

"Are you connecting this with the murder?" she asked. Fear for her own safety was almost as strong as her desire to obtain information for the newspaper.

Browning watched as the mechanic swung the damaged tires into his trunk. His thick black lashes couldn't hide from Sarah the look of concern in his eyes.

"I'm not connecting anything right now. It's strange, though, that the only damaged cars on the street were yours and mine. I just want to take a closer look at the tires, that's all. I'll be collecting yours from the tire shop tomorrow too."

He didn't tell her that he wanted to compare the size of the slash marks with the wound on Professor Lichner's back. Barone would also check out the tires and cars for fingerprints.

"Who would target you and me? If it was the murderer, what's the sense in that?" Sarah questioned.

Browning looked down at her protectively. Reminding her that a murderer's actions don't usually make sense could needlessly frighten her. He also didn't want to encourage further questions.

"Like I said before, it was probably just a kid out to make trouble, and he randomly chose our cars." He looked up and down the street. The Antler was the only open business, and he had already asked a deputy who responded to his call to see if any witnesses could be inside.

Sarah sat quietly beside him as he drove her home to the cottage. He knew she was deep in thought about the incident and found himself braced for the inevitable result—another question.

She turned to him just before he reached her driveway. "Do you think someone was trying to warn us . . . or me . . . to back off?"

He quickly reached over and put his strong hand on her knee. "I doubt it, hon. I'm guessing it was just some juvenile mischief." Without admitting that the same thought had crossed his mind, he casually asked her if she'd interviewed anyone about the murder that day.

"You're thinking that might have been the person who did it, right?" she responded. His nonchalant question didn't fool her.

He pulled the car to a stop beside the cottage. Turning in his seat, he reached over and gently caressed her cheek with a finger. "No, I don't think that's the person. But if there's the slightest possibility that someone you talked to became upset, I need to know about that."

She closed her eyes briefly, loving the feel of his hand on her face. Sighing, she looked at him, blinking slowly as she relaxed into his touch. She reached for his hand, lightly kissed his fingers and enfolded them in hers.

"I talked to Heather Bergen this morning and Beth Callison this afternoon. Callison *did* get upset when I asked about her relationship with Professor Lichner."

Browning thought back on his day. He had also talked to both women, and both had not been happy with the conversations.

"Do you plan to name them in any of your stories, Sarah?"

She released his hand and squirmed slightly in her car seat. "Callison had some personal comments about Lichner's contributions to the community that I'll quote her on. Heather Bergen didn't say anything helpful. But, you might as well know, Mark—you've confirmed for me that these people have been questioned.

I won't use their names, but I will report that a few students and a school board member have been questioned. That's a fact."

Browning leaned an elbow on the console between them. "You do realize that when there's an inference in the newspaper that certain people have been questioned, it could frighten them into refusing to speak to us anymore, right? And that could hurt our investigation?"

Sarah looked at him with a resolute expression. "I always consider that possibility when I write a story, but I honestly don't think that such a vague reference will hurt you guys."

Walking her to the front door, he kissed her on the forehead and touched her chin, lifting her face to his. "What am I going to do with you, Sarah Carpenter?" he said with a shake of the head. She smiled and kissed him good-bye, stepping inside and locking the door behind her.

He circled the cottage, making sure it was safe, before walking back to the car. Backing it down her long expanse of driveway, he stopped when he reached the darkened area by the road and turned off the engine. Switching on the police scanner, he settled in, at least for the next few hours. From this vantage point, he could keep an eye on Sarah's house, unseen by her.

He didn't want her to be alarmed by his suspicions—that her journalistic sleuthing could not only hurt their investigation, but that it could also hurt her.

*   *   *

"Tires?"

Joe Barone was standing in the doorway of Browning's office, a puzzled expression on his face.

The sheriff swallowed a lukewarm gulp of strong black coffee, reheated from a pot made six hours earlier by night shift officers. He had left Sarah's cottage about four A.M., grabbing four hours of sleep before heading to work. Too rushed to iron a dress shirt, he threw on a pair of khakis and a white polo shirt emblazoned with the department's logo.

"You don't think one could be the murder weapon, Joe?" he joked weakly. He stood and stretched his back, stiff from sitting in his car most of the night.

Walking with Barone back to the evidence room, he explained what happened the night before. "It's a long shot, I know, Joe, and we don't usually go to such lengths for something petty like a tire slashing. But it's just too much of a coincidence that the only cars hit were mine and Sarah's. We might have something bigger here. I'd like you to check for fingerprints on the tires and around the tire areas on my car and Sarah's— it's at Olsen's Tire Shop—and also compare the slash marks with Lichner's wound."

Barone rubbed his chin. "Human flesh reacts much differently to penetration than rubber, Mark. Even if it was done with the same knife, the incision could be a different size. For instance, skin contracts when the knife is removed—rubber doesn't. Probably the most I can tell you is whether the knife had one or two cutting edges. Doc says the murder weapon was a single-edged knife. We also have to remember that the murder weapon broke off against bone. Although the knife was broken at a sharp angle, it's doubtful that a busted knife could cause the damage I saw on the tires, but I'll check them out for you. And I'll try to lift some prints."

Browning stifled a yawn. "How's it going with the other evidence you collected and the stuff we brought you from the house? That raincoat is really important."

"I'm driving the coat and some other items to the state crime lab today. I should have something back within the next few days. We want to be real careful on this."

Thompson stuck his head into the evidence room. "She's baaaack," he said to Browning, mocking an ominous tone.

The sheriff put his hands on his hips, looking at the floor and shaking his head. "Not Heather again," he moaned.

Thompson folded his arms. "Yup. It's your lucky day. She told Jean that she had an appointment with you, so she's in your office. It's really a curse to be such a stud, huh?"

Barone snickered, then smothered his laugh when he saw Browning's sour expression. "I need to talk to her anyway about last night's events," he muttered, remembering that she was one of the two people that both he and Sarah had spoken to the previous day.

She was reading the framed diplomas and certificates lining Browning's office walls when he entered the room. Dressed in hip-hugging jeans and a purple midriff-baring top, she turned and began to pout when she saw him.

"You're lucky that I decided to come here today," she said in a high-pitched whine. "After the way you talked to me yesterday, I shouldn't help you anymore."

"What is it now, Heather?" he asked, stone-faced.

She sat down and crossed her legs, swinging a sandaled foot as she spoke. "I almost called you right away when I saw this last night, but I was just so mad at you! Then I decided this is pretty important, so that's why I'm here."

He sat on the edge of his desk and folded his arms. "What did you see?"

Heather looked down at the bright red polish painted on her toenails. "I saw what Matt Baker was doing to your car." She leaned forward and rubbed the embroidered emblem on his shirt with her finger. "I like your shirt," she added coyly.

Browning cleared his throat and moved to his chair, deciding that placing his desk between them would be a good idea.

"Where were you and what did you see?" he asked without emotion.

She put a finger on her lip. "Let's see. I had gotten gas for my car at the station down the street from The Antler and was pulling out when I saw Matt walking down the sidewalk toward the restaurant. He was carrying something. I thought he looked weird, so I parked on the street and watched him."

She looked at him for a reaction. Browning gave none, so she continued.

"So, he looks all around like he's making sure no one sees him, then he walks over to one car and starts poking at the tires with whatever he was carrying. He runs across the street and does the same thing to another car. He looks around again, and then runs away toward the lake."

Browning's hands were folded on his desk and he was slowly twirling his thumbs. "Tell me, how did you know it was *my* car involved?"

She pushed away a stray lock of hair that had fallen in front of her eye. "I pulled out of the parking space to go look for him and drove past the cars. I *know* what your car looks like, Sheriff. I used to see you in it all the time when I took your class."

Browning nodded. "And did you find Matt?"

She shook her head. "I think he must have parked near the lake and had left by the time I got there. I tried to help catch him. I really did."

Browning leaned on an elbow, chin in his hand. "You know how you can help us, Heather? I'd appreciate it if you allowed us to take your fingerprints."

She stopped swinging her foot. "What?" She began to laugh. "Why would you want my fingerprints?"

He stood again. "As knowledgeable as you are about criminal investigation, I'm sure you understand that it is common procedure to check out the fingerprints of anyone who was close to a murder victim. I just remembered that we forgot to ask you for yours. You might even find the process interesting, being such a good student. Do you mind?"

She uncrossed her legs and sat up straight. "I . . . guess not. I think it's a waste of your time, but . . . okay, I guess."

He walked with her to the fingerprinting area near the detectives' offices, casually explaining again that it was a normal request in such investigations. His assurances, though, failed to convince her.

"I almost feel as if I should have called a lawyer first," she said as she nervously rolled one of her fingers on an electronic screen, which scanned her prints and automatically sent them to a state filing system. "I can't believe you're doing this to me after I tried to help you."

Leading her to the reception area, he held the security door open and thanked her for the information.

"Are you going to talk to Matt Baker?" she asked angrily. "He's the one you should be fingerprinting, not me! When you finally learn that he's the killer, you'll have a lot of apologizing to do!"

She left in a huff, pulling her car keys from her back pocket and jangling them noisily.

"Sounds like she's mad at you," Jean said, never looking up from the computer keyboard she was pecking at near the reception window. "I don't think she'll be visiting you again any time soon, Sheriff."

Browning sighed and ran a hand through his hair. "I can only hope, Jean. I can only hope."

He pulled his cell phone from its jacket on his belt and signaled Thompson, who had left the station to meet with Tom Barrett of the college's finance office.

"Yeah, Sheriff," Thompson answered.

"Change of plans, Charlie. Put a hold on that meeting with Barrett and do me a favor. Swing by the marina, pick up Matt Baker and bring him back here. We need to talk to him."

He repeated Heather's information, adding, "I can't say I believe her, but let's see what Baker has to say."

Matt Baker was livid.

"I had to call my father to come down to the marina and take over for me!" he yelled at Browning. "Now he thinks I've done something wrong, and I haven't done anything!"

They were in the interrogation room, equipped with a camera to record interviews with suspects. The documentation was a valuable tool in defending the sheriff's department against charges of impropriety or civil rights violations.

"Calm down, Matt," Browning began. "We only want to ask you about something that occurred last night, but let us know at any point if you would like to have an attorney present."

Thompson interrupted. "I already explained his rights before you came in here, just in case."

Baker threw his hands up in the air. "I can't believe this! What is it that you think I did last night?"

Browning leaned against the wall and folded his arms. "Let's start another way, Matt. Where were you last night between, say, seven and ten o'clock?"

Baker looked at him with a smile of satisfaction on his face. "I was home all night long. My father can vouch for me."

Thompson sucked in a long breath. "Someone's telling us something different, Matt. We know you were in downtown Hillcrest last night."

Baker wrinkled his brow. "Well, whoever told you that is lying. I never went into town last night. Who said that I did?"

They continued to pound him with questions about his activities the night before as well as on the night of the murder. Despite having to recite his answers several times, Baker's story never wavered. Browning and Thompson stepped in to the hallway to consider their options.

"I'd like to keep him here until some of our evidence comes back, but we got nothing on him," Browning said. "What do you think?"

Thompson agreed. "I'll check with his daddy on his alibi for last night, although it ain't unusual for a parent to lie to protect their kid. We've got his fingerprints on file, right?"

Browning put his hands in his pockets and nodded. "We printed him when we brought him in on a burglary investigation a while back. I'm hoping Barone can lift some prints from the tire, although I'm not sure that incident is connected to the murder."

Thompson chewed on his toothpick. "I don't know. Someone was trying to tell you something. But it's the damage to Sarah's car I can't quite figure out, can you?"

Browning narrowed his eyes. "We both had unfriendly conversations with the same two people yesterday—Heather Bergen and Beth Callison. It wouldn't surprise me if it was one of them."

"You think Beth Callison's nutty enough to do something like that?"

"I think anyone crazy enough to commit murder is nutty enough to slash a couple tires. And I haven't ruled her out on either count."

"I agree. We got her prints?"

"I checked with Barone," Browning answered. "Everyone who works at the college or holds any position there is fingerprinted. It's their policy. They do background checks on everyone."

Browning put his hand on the interrogation room's door, ready to go back in and tell Matt Baker he was free to go—for now. "Charlie, after we take care of this, let's both go and talk to Tom Barrett. Sounds like he worked with Lichner on getting that grant. There are a couple things I'd like to ask him that Beth Callison failed to explain."

Thompson straightened his tie. "Maybe if we can get

him talking, there'll be a *lot* of things he can explain that Beth Callison didn't want to discuss. She was elected to the school board—you know how those politicians are."

Browning frowned. "Hey, watch it. Although I hate to admit it, *I'm* a politician."

His detective winked at him and walked away.

Chapter Ten

Armed with a name that her fiancé unwittingly let slip at dinner the night before, Sarah looked for Martha as soon as she arrived at the office that morning. Holly James had given her a ride to work while the tires were being replaced on her pickup.

Martha was sitting at her desk, sorting through the newspaper's mail.

"Martha, I have a question for you," Sarah began. "Have you ever heard of a guy named Matt Baker?"

Martha took off her reading glasses and rolled her eyes. "Oh, boy. What has Matt done now?"

Sarah knew the name, like *every* name in town, would be familiar to Martha. She sat down in a nearby desk chair and rolled it close to the office know-it-all. "I don't know if he's done anything, but he was a student of Professor Lichner's and might be able to tell me something about him. Do you know where I can reach him?"

Martha tilted her head up and looked at Sarah through suspicious eyes. "I know you better than that, dear," she said conspiratorially. "He's involved in this somehow, isn't he?"

Knowing she couldn't control the rumors that were sure to start spreading throughout town, Sarah told her that the police had talked to Baker after the murder.

"Another student told them that Matt has been having problems in class, but that doesn't mean anything, of course," Sarah cautioned, hoping Martha wouldn't embellish the information too much.

"Well, here's what I know about Matt," Martha began, playing with her pearl necklace. "He's been in and out of trouble since he was in high school—nothing real serious, I'm told, but his father is trying to straighten him out by getting him involved in the business. He works there now."

"What business is that?"

"Baker's Marina over in Franklin—you know, next to Empire Restaurant where we held the Christmas party last year. Does Sheriff Browning think Matt killed Professor Lichner? He always seemed like a good boy at heart to me."

Sarah put her hand on Martha's arm. "I don't know what the police are thinking, Martha. That's kind of what I want to talk to Matt about. Thanks for the information. I knew I could count on you. Keep your ears open for me!"

Walking back to the empty newsroom, Sarah knew that Martha was probably already on the phone, spreading the news that police had talked to Baker. Mark would be furious when the gossip reached him. But, she justified to herself, it wasn't her job to keep a lid on information affecting the community. She just needed to be very careful when it was in print, knowing she couldn't name Matt as a suspect just yet.

Hoping he would be at work, she found the phone number for the marina and dialed it. A male voice answered, and Sarah asked for Matt Baker.

"Speaking. How can I help you?"

"Hi, Matt. My name is Sarah Carpenter, and I'm editor of the *Potter County Times.* I understand that you were a student of Professor Lichner's, and I'm wondering if you have a minute to talk to me about him."

Baker hesitated. "Ah . . . why do you want to talk to *me*? He had lots of students."

Doing a sensitive interview required fast thinking. A question had to be worded in such a way that useful information was obtained without scaring away the person.

"Well, your name came up in a conversation I had with one of the investigating officers," Sarah told him. Getting the interviewee mad at the police wasn't a bad tactic, either. Sometimes the lips got looser.

"I'm guessing you have some information about him that might be important to the story," she continued.

"The cops told you they talked to me? They're trying to pin something on me that I had nothing to do with!"

Sarah needed to calm him down without stopping his

obvious willingness to talk. "No, no. They didn't name you as a suspect. I'm just wondering why they talked to you in the first place. Do you have any idea why Lichner might have been killed?"

Baker heaved a disgusted sigh. "They told me they're checking out students who were failing his class, but I know they're looking at me because I got into some minor trouble in the past. But, murder? That ain't my bag, man. This won't get in the paper, will it?"

Sarah told him the truth, hoping it would encourage him to talk even more. "In a criminal investigation, we only print the names of people who have been charged, unless there are special circumstances with a witness or something. But, no, there's no need to identify you in the paper at this time, Matt."

He opened up. "Get a load of this one—I just got back from the cop shop because they think I might have slashed the sheriff's tires last night! Can you believe it? It's like they're going to blame everything on me now."

Sarah would add that to her next story—that one person had been questioned in connection with both the murder and the tire incident. *But why would Matt Baker slash my tires? Did he target Mark and just add my car to make it look like random vandalism?*

"But the police let you go, so do they think someone else did the tires?" she asked.

"Who knows? They know I was at home with my dad all night, so they got nothing to go on."

Sarah turned the conversation back to the murder.

"Who do you think the police are looking at for the murder, Matt?"

He snorted. "Heck if I know. I told them I thought Lichner might be involved in something fishy because of all the spending he'd been doing lately."

Sarah scribbled furiously as he recounted the various purchases Lichner's students had noticed in recent months.

"And," he continued, "they should check into that school board broad—her name's Callison or something. Everyone knew they were dating, and then all of a sudden they'd pass each other on campus and not say a word. I wouldn't be surprised if she's the one who put the cops on to me. I'm sure Lichner told her all about his 'problem children,'" he added bitterly.

Sarah raised an eyebrow. "You think she gave them your name?"

He backed off slightly. "I don't know—they probably just found out I was in the class and fingered me as the troublemaker." Suddenly ending the conversation, he said, "I probably shouldn't be talking to you. I don't want to screw anything up for the cops."

And he hung up.

Sarah slowly lowered the phone, wondering why Baker clammed up after mentioning Beth Callison. Her thoughts were interrupted when an excited Martha entered the newsroom with clasped hands and a flushed face.

"Don't accuse Matt Baker of the murder just yet, honey. I know who else might have done it!"

Sarah smiled. "What's the word on the street now, Martha?"

She patted her curls nervously and sat in Holly's chair, anxious to tell Sarah her news.

"I just happened to be talking to Alma a few minutes ago, and we somehow got on the topic of Professor Lichner. Well, Alma's in the historical society, too, and she had breakfast today with one of the other girls in the club. I'm not supposed to tell you her name, but guess what this girl saw after a society meeting a few weeks ago?"

She looked at Sarah with wide eyes, extending the drama of her story.

Sarah shook her head and held her hands palms up. "I can't guess!"

Martha leaned toward Sarah. "She was on clean-up duty after the meeting, so she left after everyone else. She said when she was walking to her car, she noticed that the professor's car was still in the parking lot. He had a BMW, by the way. Anyway, she saw another car parked on the street, and two people were sitting in it arguing at the top of their lungs. She could hear them even with the windows closed! And, guess who they were?"

Martha waited for Sarah's response.

"I don't know! Who?" Sarah said impatiently.

"Professor Lichner and Beth Callison!"

Sarah leaned back against her chair, tapping her chin with an index finger. "Hmm. That *is* pretty interesting. They had already broken up a while before that. I wonder what they were fighting about."

"Well, Dorothy—oh, I wasn't supposed to say her name—anyway, Dorothy said she couldn't hear what they were talking about and didn't want to stare, so she got in her car and drove away. But, she said they seemed very angry."

It wasn't information she could use in her story, but hearing Beth Callison's name twice in consecutive conversations was curious, Sarah thought. It was time to ask the school board president some more questions, which Sarah knew would draw an angry response.

But making someone angry—even her own fiancé—had never stopped Sarah from doing her job.

Tom Barrett was logging numbers into a spreadsheet on his computer when Browning and Thompson knocked on his office door. Looking up and recognizing the men he had spoken to just two days before, he offered them a seat.

"I was going to give you a call," he told them. "You asked me to try to think of something that might be helpful to you. Is that why you're here?"

Browning nodded. "That's one reason. Do you have some information for us?"

Barrett swung his seat away from his computer and folded his hands on his desk. "I could think of only one thing. I probably wasn't as forthright as I should have been with you when discussing Philip's relationship with Beth Callison. I'm the type who is uncomfortable talking about other people's personal business, but now I realize that this isn't the time to be discreet.

"I know that the two of them were having problems, but I just don't know what caused them. Talk around school was that she's the bossy type, and he just didn't want to deal with her ego anymore. I don't know if that's true."

Thompson gnawed on his toothpick, waiting for Barrett to elaborate. He didn't.

"That's it? That's all you can think of?" he asked.

Barrett shrugged apologetically. "Like I said, I didn't know him well. I should have told you earlier what the talk around campus was, though."

Browning raised a finger. "Speaking of not knowing him well, we've been told that you have been at Professor Lichner's house. Why would you go to his house if you two weren't friendly?"

Barrett looked confused. "I was at his house? Oh, do you mean when I dropped off some paperwork? I was barely there for two minutes, and it was work-related." A look of understanding passed over his face. "That's right. Beth Callison must have told you this, because she was arriving just as I was leaving. Well, doesn't *she* have quite the memory!"

"What kind of paperwork would involve both you and Professor Lichner?" Browning asked.

He glanced at the piles of documents on his desk. "I believe it was information he needed for a grant he was working on—an historic preservation grant. We eventually received it, and it's been very helpful in our renovation project here at the college."

"And what kind of information did he need?" the sheriff asked.

Barrett raised his eyes upward in thought. "He needed financial figures regarding our project—how much it would cost, what our budget was, etcetera, etcetera. I had the information because I'm the project manager as well as the school's finance officer."

Thompson smoothed his tie over his belly. "The project ain't doing so well, huh, Mr. Barrett?"

He looked at Thompson with a disgusted expression. "That is an opinion I don't happen to share. The school board was in entire agreement on the costs until some taxpayers began to complain. Then, the board changed its tone and I've been singled out as the scapegoat. I have reminded the board members time and time again that they approved all the bids for the renovation work on the buildings."

"Beth Callison says the board is unhappy with the quality of the work—that they expected a better job for the money," Browning interjected.

Barrett began to speak, then stopped, then began again. "This is a difficult topic for me, as you can see. The board was not aware of the costs involved in the renovation of historic landmarks. I recommended at first that we do the job right and raise our budget for quality work, possibly applying for more grants and even going to the public to request a tax rate increase. But the board rejected that and kept our project's budget to the bare minimum. Thank God for the grant—it gave us a little more money to put toward items like façade repairs and window restoration."

Browning tapped his pen on the notebook in his lap. "Mr. Barrett, we'll need all the documents related to the renovation project. Can you provide them to us now?"

Barrett stared at him briefly, his mouth tight. "You're investigating Philip Lichner's murder," he said flatly. "For what possible reason do you need information regarding the building project?"

"It's pretty simple, sir," Browning answered, slightly annoyed at being questioned about his request. "We need to know what our victim was involved with before his death. Obviously, the project was one of his recent activities. We want all information related to it."

Barrett began to drum his fingers on his desk. "Well, it will take me a few days to get all the documents together for you. You don't understand—there's a myriad amount of paperwork that is involved with such a huge undertaking as this. Why, it could take—"

Thompson interrupted. "How about that file sitting on your cabinet marked Renovation Project, sir? Looks ready to me," he said bluntly, cracking a new stick of gum he had just softened in his mouth, and pointing to the folder.

Barrett looked at it, flustered. "There's no order to that file. That's just where I'd throw a copy of a document once I'd filed the original in the proper location and put the information on my computer. You won't be able to make any sense out of it."

Browning stood and picked up the folder. "Tell you what, Mr. Barrett, we'll take this with us and you can get to work on putting together information in any order you like. We'll expect it in a day or two."

Barrett leaned his elbows on his desk, looking at Browning with intense blue eyes. "I realize you need that information, but this whole controversy has been a nightmare for me after all my hard work. I just don't want you to misread what's been done in the project and start pointing fingers at me all over again. I've really been treated unfairly. The board needs to take responsibility for its actions."

Browning tucked the thick file under his arm. "I'm not interested in whether the project was a failure or who is to blame. I'm interested in who killed Professor Lichner. Will this information help us? I have no idea. But it's worth looking at."

Thompson straightened up in his chair. "One more question before we let you get to work on compiling that information, Mr. Barrett. Did you notice any unusual purchases the professor made lately? Like, expensive purchases?"

Barrett slowly shook his head. "No, nothing that comes to mind. I didn't see anything out of the ordinary when I was at his house. I mean, it was a nice house and all, but not ostentatious."

"You didn't notice, say, a new car or anything like that?" Thompson asked.

"I have no idea what kind of car Philip drove, ever," Barrett answered.

The men soon thanked Barrett and left, armed with a load of financial information that made Thompson groan.

"I hate numbers," he growled, leafing through the file as they drove back to the department. "Give me a murder—I'll solve it. Give me a math test—I'll flunk."

Chapter Eleven

A voice mail from Ken McCarthy, president of the Potter County Board of Commissioners, was waiting for Browning when he returned to his office. McCarthy rarely interfered in department business, so the message could mean only one thing—he was worried about the murder investigation.

"Hello, Ken," Browning said when McCarthy, a lawyer in his full-time career, answered his phone. "I got your message. What's up?"

McCarthy engaged in small talk before getting to the real point of his phone call. "The murder, Mark— how's the investigation going?"

McCarthy and the rest of the county board were Browning's bosses. While his inclination was to tell McCarthy that the investigation was private police business, Browning knew that wasn't the politically smart thing to do. He decided to throw him a few crumbs to chew on.

"We're talking to a few people we're interested in, Ken—a couple of students and some people Lichner worked with. We've also collected some evidence that might lead us in the right direction."

McCarthy exhaled and Browning could tell he was contemplating his next question.

"I got a call from Beth Callison, Mark. She's pretty upset. She says you and Detective Thompson have been hounding her and that you've even suggested to the newspaper—and by that I assume she means Sarah—that she might be involved in this."

Browning tightened his grip on the phone. He was steamed. "First of all, Ken, Charlie and I aren't 'hounding' her. We talked to her one time, which is pretty damn understandable since she was Lichner's girlfriend. And second, Sarah's pretty good at finding people to talk to all on her own. We didn't tell her a thing about Beth Callison."

"C'mon, Mark. Beth Callison? She's our library director and the president of the college board. You think she's capable of murder?"

Browning exhaled loudly. "I've seen people from all walks of life who were capable of murder, and I'm not eliminating anyone from our list based simply on who they are. Is that what you're telling me to do, Ken? Because it's not going to happen."

McCarthy was silent for a moment. "Listen, Mark. The school board is taking enough heat already because of the screwed up building project. Now, one of our community leaders could be wrongly accused of murder. My job is to keep our county a place where people want to live and do business. This sure doesn't help."

Browning didn't back down. "Ken, you've got your job and I've got mine. Odds are, we're going to butt heads a couple of times down the line. But I made it clear when I ran for this position that I wouldn't let political realities get in the way of my job. If that happens, I'm stepping down."

McCarthy wouldn't let that happen—Mark Browning was the most capable and popular sheriff the county had ever seen.

"All right, Mark. I guess I'll just have to trust your instincts. I want you to be aware, though, of what we're hearing on our end."

Browning ended the conversation, half-heartedly thanking him for the information, before finding Thompson to let him know they needed to talk to Beth Callison again.

Sarah's phone rang after she talked to Martha. It was Mr. Jakes, asking her to come up to his office.

"Come in, Sarah," he said when she rapped on his door. "I need to talk to you about a phone call I just received."

She held up a hand. "Let me guess. Someone else complaining about me marrying the sheriff, right?"

Jakes adjusted his bow tie. "Ah . . . not in so many words, but I'm sure that's part of it. Ken McCarthy called me. He said he received a complaint from Beth Callison that you are harassing her, and she thinks Sheriff Browning put you up to it."

Sarah looked up at the ceiling, shaking her head. "Mr. Jakes, the *last* thing Mark would do is to set me loose on a possible murder suspect."

Jakes appeared to be stunned. "Beth Callison is a suspect in the murder?"

"Mark . . . er . . . the sheriff says that no one is considered a suspect at this time, but Callison is Professor Lichner's former girlfriend, and she has been questioned by the police. That is why I talked to her. I try to talk to everyone who might have information for my story."

Jakes rocked back and forth in his swivel chair. "But, is it fair to put someone in Beth Callison's position in such an unfavorable light? After all, she's one of our finest citizens. Will you be naming her in the story and discussing her personal relationship with Lichner?"

Sarah folded her arms. Her publisher's concerns about losing advertisers were becoming apparent. "At this time, I think we could be risking legal action if I use her name. I *will* be printing that police have talked to a school board member. I can't control what our readers will conclude from that."

She waited for Jakes' reaction with apprehension. His loyalty to the business side of the newspaper was stronger than his devotion to the news side.

Jakes slapped his palm on his desk. "That sounds fine to me. I must admit that I get a little tired of those county board members trying to tell me what we can or can't print in my newspaper!"

Sarah felt like hugging him.

Martha was looking for Sarah just as she returned to the newsroom.

"Oh, there you are, dear. I answered your phone while you were away, and it's your fiancé. Gosh, I love that deep voice of his!"

Sarah smiled and picked up her phone. "Hi, there, sexy voice."

"Huh?"

She laughed. "Never mind. I was just going to call you, but you go first."

"Just a little warning," he told her. "It sounds like Beth Callison has been calling the powers-that-be to complain about you. Hon, it's best if you just wait to do your investigative reporter routine until we pin down a serious suspect. I don't want to see you get in trouble."

Sarah was taken aback. Was Mark telling her to lay off the story? "In trouble with whom? With Ken McCarthy? With Beth Callison? Or with you? And what do you mean by 'my investigative reporter routine?' "

Browning knew he'd entered sensitive territory. He didn't like her putting out information that could interfere with his work, but his greatest concern was that her actions could place her in danger. Someone had struck out at them already—he didn't want something worse to happen.

"I'm just saying that you don't want to report inaccurate information, Sarah. It could cause all kinds of trouble for everyone."

"But, Mark, you leave me no other alternative than to seek out the information on my own because you refuse to talk about what you're doing! If you want correct information to be reported, then you have to give it to me."

Browning rubbed his forehead, frustrated. Like always, this argument was going nowhere.

Sarah continued. "I was going to call you because I'd like to know why Beth Callison thinks everyone is harassing her. Are you focusing on her as a suspect now? Is that why she's so upset?"

He hesitated before answering, tempted to tell her that Callison was among a few people who could honestly be classified as suspects. He wanted to warn her to stay away from all of them, revealing their names, but that could jeopardize the entire investigation.

She practically read his mind. "Mark, I know who you've been talking to. Just point me in the right direction. Tell me what your gut says."

He exhaled loudly. "Can't do that, kiddo," he said quietly. "Just trust me when I tell you to be very careful."

When they ended the phone call, Mark had the unsettled feeling that she wouldn't listen to his warning.

*   *   *

Sarah knew what Mark was trying to tell her. He always worried that she'd poke her nose into places where she didn't belong. Past experiences taught him that. She'd never shied away from possible trouble.

But she had never been a reporter who was satisfied with the standard lines issued by police types. Her readers deserved more, she believed, from the people who were supposed to protect them. If she couldn't get the truth from the police, she'd get it herself.

That's why she picked up the phone to call Callison. She wanted to know what prompted the woman to lash out at both the police and the newspaper. And, she needed to dispel Callison's notion that the *Times* was in the back pocket of the sheriff's department. That was an insult she wouldn't let pass.

She opened the conversation with close to an apology, hoping to soften Callison into not immediately hanging up on her.

"Beth, this is Sarah Carpenter calling in hopes that I can straighten out what seems to be a misunderstanding concerning my last conversation with you," she said quickly when Callison answered her phone.

She'd actually written that down before dialing the number, knowing that the success of the phone call depended on her first words. An opener like, "Hi. This is Sarah Carpenter," would surely have ended in failure.

"A misunderstanding? What are you talking about?" Callison asked.

So far, so good.

"My publisher received a phone call from Ken McCarthy. We've been told that you feel the sheriff's department might have . . . well . . . led me to believe that you were a person who should be questioned about Professor Lichner's murder. I just want you to know that's entirely untrue."

"Well, you *are* marrying the sheriff, aren't you? What else am I supposed to think when the two of you both start asking me the same questions?"

Sarah kept her composure. "Yes, I know how you could reach that conclusion. It *is* a unique situation. But it is important to me for both my readers and my sources to know that Sheriff Browning and I do not share information regarding police cases. I learned of your relationship with Professor Lichner on my own— you can certainly understand why I would want to talk to you."

"Do you realize what an awkward position you have put me in?" Callison responded in a still angry, but less strident voice. "My staff saw me questioned by both the police and the newspaper in the same day. You can just imagine what people are saying about me! And this comes on top of the building project controversy! It's just been an awful week. I would like for all of this to just go away."

Sarah picked up on her last comment. It was said in a tone of helplessness, as if Callison needed to reach out to someone for help.

"I can understand how hard it's been. Did the police give you any hope that they're close to solving this?"

Callison's voice rose again. "Absolutely not! Like I told Ken McCarthy, they made me feel as if I'm a suspect! I refuse to talk to them again until they apologize for their behavior. And, I'm sorry Sarah, that includes your fiancé."

Sarah sensed a definite change in Callison's attitude—she was opening up to Sarah and painting the police as the bad guys. Briefly wondering if she was ready to propose this kind of story idea, she decided to go for it.

"Beth, how would you like to sit down with me and tell me your side of the story? I mean, for print. You're worried about public perception of you following these recent events—this would be your chance to clear the air."

Sarah knew the story could be a risky endeavor. Callison could lie throughout their interview—those lies would be reported in the paper. And, Sarah had told Mr. Jakes that Callison's name would not be printed—but it would be. Worst of all, Callison could be a murderer—and Sarah would be presenting her as a victim.

On the other hand, Sarah would make it clear to her readers that the story was intended only to present Callison's side of the story. She would include that police had no comment on her possible involvement in the murder. Readers, as usual, could draw their own conclusions.

Sarah waited as Callison mulled the idea for at least

a minute, sighing several times as she considered it. Her words suddenly spilled out in a fury.

"There are so many things I'd like to talk about, and I'm so tired of keeping them inside of me," she choked through hot tears. "The building project, what happened with Philip—it's just been too much! Maybe this *is* the best route for me to go, through the newspaper. I'm ready to . . . to let everything out, but I'm so afraid the police will just twist my words and continue to hold everything against me!"

Sarah was uncomfortable with Callison's sudden emotion. It hurt to know that she was putting the woman in such a difficult position, but Sarah reminded herself that she could not let her feelings stand in the way of telling the story.

They agreed to meet the next evening after the library closed for the night. Sarah knew she should have been overjoyed that she'd convinced Callison to talk to her, but instead, she felt some trepidation. She tried to ignore the gnawing feeling that Callison's emotional outburst could be the sign of a dangerous woman.

And Callison's words—*"what happened with Philip"*—kept spinning through her mind. Was she going to tell her?

"Can I ask a favor?"

Sarah had called Mark after learning that tires needed to be ordered for her pickup. She wouldn't have her vehicle back until the next day, and she needed a ride home from work.

"Oh, I get it," Mark said with a laugh in his voice. "Don't take my advice on your stories, but you won't turn down a ride, huh?"

She smiled. "How about I pay you back with a home-made dinner?" she asked meekly.

"It's a deal. I'll pick you up in twenty minutes."

Soon, they were in her cottage. Mark sat at her small antique kitchen table with hand-painted designs, feet propped up on a nearby chair while she cooked. He inhaled the appetizing smells of an Italian sausage, potatoes and peppers medley, one of his favorite meals. A Lake Michigan breeze from an open kitchen window mellowed the accompanying fragrance of garlic.

Sarah promised to herself on the drive home that she would not bring up the subject of Philip Lichner's death. He needed a break from it and so did she. They needed to remember to focus on each other, she decided, not just on their jobs. And she didn't want Mark to know who she planned to meet with the next night.

Instead, they talked about the wedding.

"When are you going to buy your new suit?" Sarah asked. He had been immensely relieved when she agreed with him that a tuxedo could be uncomfortable at an outdoor reception, particularly if their June day happened to be hot.

He swallowed a mouthful of the savory sausage and sipped a glass of red wine. "Soon. And you'll be happy to know that Charlie's wife, Anne, will be helping him pick out his best man suit. So, don't worry, everything he wears will match. He's even getting a new tie."

Sarah laughed and took a bite of garlic bread. She and her sister, Gretchen, were planning a weekend shopping trip to Chicago soon to find the perfect matron-of-honor dress.

"How about you go put your dress on for me now so I can see it?" Browning asked with a wink.

Sarah pretended to be shocked. "That's bad luck! You're not supposed to see me until I walk down the aisle!"

"Aw, c'mon. One little look. You don't even have to put it on. I need to know what it looks like so I can pick out the right kind of suit."

She was just as anxious to show it to him as he was to see it. "All right." She rinsed her garlic-laden fingers under the kitchen faucet. "I'll go get it."

She retrieved it from its protected place in her closet and carefully carried it by its padded hanger to the kitchen door.

"Here it is," she said quietly, holding it against her with her free arm and waiting for his reaction.

Browning turned, his eyes softening as they traveled up and down its satin curves. Sarah felt a lump form in her throat when she noticed Mark's eyes moisten just a bit.

"It's perfect, hon, just like you," he said simply.

Later, they curled up on the couch together and watched an old movie late into the night. Browning kissed her slowly as they said good-bye, holding her for a long time before heading out the door to his lonely apartment. It was a nice ending to a rough day, Sarah thought.

And they hadn't mentioned Lichner all night.

Chapter Twelve

Browning got his first full night's sleep since the murder. He was relieved that Sarah hadn't wanted to discuss the case the night before. Maybe she'd taken his advice, he thought, and decided to leave it alone until they were ready to arrest someone. He felt they were getting closer.

He padded across the apartment's cold linoleum floors and into his tiny kitchen, clad only in pajama pants. Dropping two pieces of cinnamon raisin bread into the toaster, he took a long swig from the carton of orange juice he'd grabbed from the refrigerator. He reminded himself that he'd have to break that habit once he moved in with Sarah.

Browning sat at the retro formica table near the kitchen window. While buttering his pieces of toast, he glanced at yesterday's copy of the *Times* on the table. Too busy the day before to read Sarah's story on the murder, he opened the folded broadsheet newspaper and took a look at the front page.

The corners of his eyes crinkled in amusement when he read what Sarah had quoted from him.

"I can only confirm that the victim is Professor Philip Lichner," said Sheriff Mark Browning. "Our investigation is continuing."

He knew she included the quote to tell readers that police were being close-mouthed, but he'd never operate any other way. Reading on, he saw she had named a knife as the murder weapon, but left out the detail on its size. That was good. But he winced when he saw she got close to naming who they'd been talking to.

Police are looking into reports that Lichner may have had problems with at least one of his students. They are also interviewing colleagues of the professor.

It wasn't specific information, but he would have preferred that Sarah not mention that angle of the investigation. All in all, though, the story seemed harmless. He was curious what she'd be reporting in the next issue. Nothing about Beth Callison, he hoped.

Browning felt that it was a good idea to dress like his deputies every now and then—in uniform. After showering and shaving, he began the time-consuming process of attaching the various requisite pins and badges to his white uniform shirt. He pulled it on and stepped into his French-blue uniform pants with navy-blue stripes on the sides. Adjusting the light blue clip-on tie and attaching his gun and holster to his belt, he was almost ready to go. He grabbed his pager and cell phone off his dresser and added them to his belt accessories. When on a call, he'd also carry a portable radio on his hip. *No wonder so many cops have back problems,* he thought.

Browning quickly thumbed through the thick file that they had taken from Tom Barrett's office, mentally dividing the paperwork into categories he could analyze more easily. Scanning each page, he would drop it into one of several piles that were growing on his desk. Each pile represented a different aspect of the project's planning and costs. He didn't quite know what he was looking for. He just knew that he wanted to find more information regarding Lichner's work on the historic preservation grant.

By the time he'd gotten to the last piece of paperwork in the file, he'd created about ten separate piles of documents. One contained legal notices for work bid requests, another contained the bid specifications, others contained budget guidelines, and more held lists of the winning contractors' bids on various aspects of the renovation.

Browning glanced over each pile. The one with information on the grant would need to be looked at closely. He also wanted to double-check the costs of the work with Barrett. He looked for a stack containing contractors' final bills and couldn't find it. That must be some of the information that Barrett told them wasn't included in the file, he decided. He picked up the phone to call him.

"Well, I know that file contains the bids from each contractor, Sheriff," Barrett told him. "Add those together, and that will give you a general idea of the total cost of the work. It didn't vary much. In fact, much of the work came in less than what had been bid."

A "general idea" wasn't good enough for Browning. "I want the exact amount of the final cost, Mr. Barrett. I know you're putting together more information for us—please include the final bills that were submitted to the college."

Barrett sighed. "That will take a while to compile," he said curtly. "I'll do my best."

Browning told him he'd stop by the school the next morning to collect the documents, then stood up to stretch and rub his eyes. He hated looking at numbers almost as much as Thompson.

Heading back from the lunch room after pouring himself a cup of coffee, he saw Barone hanging around his office door.

"Mark!" Barone called to him as he headed down the hallway. "I got something for you!"

"Results on the raincoat already?"

"No, sorry. The state crime lab's still working on that stuff, but I got a hit on fingerprints I lifted on those tires."

It was the lesser of Browning's concerns, but still good news. Barone followed him into the office and laid fingerprint photos on his desk.

"Congratulate me—it's not easy to get prints off a tire. But this is what we got from the electronic prints off Livescan and this is what I managed to lift from a tire on each car. I got prints off your car too." Barone pointed to the pictures. "See the matching points?"

The prints Barone lifted weren't as clear as the scanned prints, but the match was obvious. He looked up at Barone.

"Who do they belong to?"

Barone responded almost in disbelief. "Heather Bergen."

Browning whistled softly through his teeth. "Heather Bergen, well, well, well."

Thompson poked his head in the doorway. "Hey, boss. Hey, Joe. What's up?"

Browning pointed to the prints on his desk. "Get this. The job on my tires the other night—guess who did it? Heather Bergen."

Thompson popped his gum. "You mentioned her as one of the maybes, didn't you? Surprised?"

Browning scratched the back of his head. "Everything pointed to her as a possibility, but I guess I didn't think she really had it in her. You think we got a link here to the murder?"

Thompson shrugged. "Maybe she ain't the sweet little girl she makes herself out to be. Remember, she lied to us and tried to pin this on Matt Baker. She's been naming that kid from the start."

Browning nodded. "Let's bring her in and talk to her here, Charlie. We'll check with the school to see if she has a class and pick her up there."

Thompson stepped over to the desk and peered at the prints. "Well, I guess she got her wish. Looks like she'll be spending a lot more time with you, but maybe not in the way she'd like."

Heather was in tears when they sat her in the inter-rogation room. She'd been advised of her rights and strongly urged to get an attorney.

"Call your parents if you have to, Heather," Browning told her. "I really think it would be a good move to have a lawyer with you right now."

"No, I don't need one!" she insisted with a stomp of her foot. "I don't know how those fingerprints got there. Maybe Matt Baker planted them somehow!"

Thompson rolled his eyes. "Listen, kid, we're done playing around with you. This is serious business. What's going on here?"

She looked at Browning, mascara smeared under her wet eyes. "Mark, you believe me, don't you? I've been trying to help you! Why would I do something like that?"

He responded bluntly. "Heather, we're already going to charge you with criminal damage to property, got it? Like Detective Thompson said, this is serious business.

You've just gotten yourself involved in our murder investigation, and you've got some explaining to do. For instance, tell me again why you were on campus the night of Professor Lichner's murder. Your class with him ended two hours earlier."

She wiped her runny mascara with an index finger. "I told you—I was in the library doing some research. Can't you see that Matt killed him? It's so obvious! If only you'd let me talk to him, we could solve this together. We'd—"

Browning interrupted her. "Heather, do you know who Sarah Carpenter is?"

She looked at him with narrowed eyes and wrinkled her nose in distaste. "No! Why? Should I?"

He shrugged. "Maybe. Do you know that I have a girlfriend?"

Thompson watched Heather closely as Browning fired questions at her. He knew what his boss was doing.

She clicked her tongue. "Why should I care?" she spat out, looking at everything except Browning.

"Do you know I'm getting married soon?"

She bolted from her chair and headed for the door. Thompson blocked her way and grabbed her arm.

"Sit down, kid," he told her gruffly. She frowned at him and pulled her arm from his grip, finally complying with his order.

"Why did those questions upset you, Heather?" Browning said, sitting down on the edge of the table in front of her.

She leaned toward him with an insolent face. "Because they were so stupid! Why should I care about your love life?"

"You shouldn't."

More questions produced the same answers from Heather, and the men let her sit inside the room while they stepped into the hallway to talk.

"What do you think, Charlie?" Browning said as he pulled the door shut. "Can we hold her on more than the CDP charge? I'm thinking we don't have enough on her yet."

Thompson agreed. "The criminal damage charge might keep her locked up until mommy or daddy bring in her bond money. But we got nothin' else."

Browning nodded. "I'll grab a deputy to watch her while we take care of the paperwork."

As they walked down the hallway, Thompson began to shake his head in mock despair. "Poor kid," he moaned. "How could you go and break her heart like that?" Browning responded with a dirty look.

Less than two hours later, after the charge against her had been filed and she'd placed a tearful call to her mother, Heather left the station.

Sarah hung up the phone and sat back in her chair, absorbing what Mark had just called to tell her—that they had charged Heather with the damage on their cars. He had cautioned her that police were not tying it in to the murder, but Sarah knew better. The timing of the two incidents, and the fact that one of the cars belonged to an investigating officer, was just too strange. She would print only the facts of the arrest in the next issue, but run that story near her murder investigation update.

Mark had asked her if she still had the note someone left a few nights before on her cottage porch. Without elaborating further, he told her he might have it checked for fingerprints. She had returned it to its envelope, and it still sat on her rolltop desk, she told him. He said he would pick it up that night.

She wondered what he was thinking. Heather most definitely had a crush on Mark, she knew. Her behavior around him the night of the murder and the way she talked about him in her phone conversation with Sarah made that obvious. Had jealousy prompted the actions that Mark suspected her of? And why was he treating these relatively minor incidents so seriously? She put these thoughts on her list of questions to ask Mark when she saw him later that night, after meeting with Beth Callison.

The Hillcrest Public Library was closed two nights during the week due to a tight budget. Callison had asked Sarah to meet with her there at six o'clock, about an hour after all staff members should have gone home. She wanted no one to see her meeting with the *Times* editor. It would be hard enough talking about the matters at hand, she had said—a library full of nosy colleagues would make it worse.

Sarah spent her day editing wedding and engagement announcements and writing two editorials for the weekend issue. One dealt with the building renovation controversy at the college. Because of taxpayer questions on the results, the *Times* called for the school board to provide a full accounting of the costs involved. Sarah scolded the board for dodging taxpayer requests for information and warned that their positions could be in jeopardy in the next election.

She was glad the editorial would run *after* her meeting with Callison.

Her stomach growled noisily as she pulled on the lightweight suede jacket she'd brought to work that morning when a springtime chill returned to the area. She checked her watch—still time to stop for a bite to eat before heading to the library.

A small takeout hot dog place was conveniently located next door to the newspaper office. She ordered her usual—the Chicago Special—which included fries and a hot dog with mustard, chopped onions, a garlic pickle spear and celery salt. Adding ketchup was considered a regional sin.

Holly had given her a ride to work that morning, and the tire shop owner was kind enough to drop off the pickup at the office after new tires had been installed. And when she saw the traces of powdery residue near the wheel wells, she knew Mark must have ordered fingerprint testing on her truck too. It gave her an uneasy feeling as she slid behind the steering wheel.

As she drove the few miles to the library, she noted that the area's huge oak and maple trees were in full leafy splendor as the calendar quickly approached

May. It wouldn't be too long now before she wouldn't have to say good-bye to Mark each night at her door.

She pulled into the parking lot of the library, set just on the outskirts of Hillcrest's oldest neighborhood. Stately Victorians and charming Queen Annes mixed with other architectural styles popular in the periods after Hillcrest was established. This neighborhood, she remembered, was where Professor Lichner had lived.

The lot was empty except for one car that Sarah assumed was Callison's. Under an overcast sky in fading evening sun, she could see that only a few security lights were on in the building. Callison had told her that the front door would be open—she said she'd tell the staff that she was working late and would lock up before leaving.

Walking past the ornamental grasses that were just beginning to come to life in the library's landscaping, Sarah felt a slight shiver as the isolation of the meeting place became evident. No cars passed on the street, and the few houses nearby showed no signs of life. Inside waiting for her was a person who had made it clear that she was going to reveal difficult information, and she didn't know what kind of emotional state this person would be in. Unconsciously, Sarah's grip on her notebook tightened.

The automatic front doors slid open when Sarah reached them. Inside the foyer, she passed a bronze statue of an elderly woman reading a book to a child. The main room, usually bustling with people browsing through the shelves or checking out a book at the busy circulation desk, was strangely quiet.

Sarah had anticipated that Callison would meet her at the front desk, but figured she must have decided to remain in her office. *Probably didn't want to take the chance of someone seeing me with her through the front doors.*

She stepped behind the desk and walked down a rear hallway toward Callison's office. Seeing a light spilling from its door, she stepped inside. Callison was not there.

Puzzled, Sarah stepped back into the hallway. If she had changed her mind about the meeting, Sarah thought, she would have locked up the library and left. She must still be somewhere inside, maybe finishing up some work from the day, Sarah decided.

The hallway led out to the rear of the main room, behind the rows of shelves that held the library's modest collection of books. Sarah slowly walked along the rear wall, looking down each row as she passed. Could Callison be shelving books that hadn't been returned to their proper place by the end of the day? Could she be looking for a book of her own to bring home?

A large smudge on the wall near a hall leading to the rear exit froze her in her tracks. She looked at it closely. A surge of adrenaline coursed through her body and her heart began to pound when she recognized its source—blood.

Then she saw the rest of it.

The carpeted floor of the hall leading to her right was covered with dark droplets. Turning the corner, she saw the exit door smeared with it. It was blood, and the rivulets that flowed down the door to the floor led to Callison.

Turning her back to the horrifying scene and feeling as if the wind had been knocked out of her, she pulled her cell phone from her jacket pocket and dialed the sheriff's department.

Chapter Thirteen

Discovering a second bloodied body so soon after the first was almost too much for Sarah to bear.

"Beth Callison . . . at the library . . . I think she's been murdered," she croaked into the phone, barely managing to find her voice. In robotic fashion, she answered the dispatcher's questions before her weakened knees gave way and she sank to the floor.

She held her swooning head in her hand for a moment, waiting for the faint feeling of nausea to pass. With eyes closed, she waited anxiously for the sound of sirens—for the sound of help.

She raised her head and opened her eyes, seeing again the lifeless form of Callison lying face up. Her arm was flung across her face, the other twisted beneath her head. Her white blouse was half-soaked in blood.

A sudden feeling of fear overcame her shock. *I can't stay here, the killer could still be inside the building!*

She tried to stand quickly. Her trembling limbs were not cooperating, and she started to crawl awkwardly next to the rear wall of the main room. Stopping to lean her shoulder against the wall, she finally found the strength to stand and start moving her legs toward the library's front entrance.

One by one, she passed the shelves of books, fearing that the next row would reveal the killer hiding there. She stepped into the hallway, still illuminated by the light from Callison's office. Approaching it slowly, she bit her lip as she reached the door, almost afraid to glance inside. It was empty.

She knew that she should run from the building, but a folder on Callison's otherwise spotless desk drew her to it. Her reporter's instincts had fought their way to the surface. Ignoring the eerie feeling that enveloped her as she sat down in Callison's chair, Sarah opened the folder with a shaking hand, revealing what appeared to be several invoices and other financial documents.

Hearing sirens approaching the library, she scanned the pages quickly. Numerous bills described work done at the college. Other documents detailed the minutes of school board meetings. More papers looked like typical bid submissions made by companies looking to do a job. All seemed to be related to the renovation project at the school.

Sarah thought back to her conversation with

Callison. She had mentioned wanting to talk about the project as well as the murder of Philip Lichner. Both subjects were a source of pain for her, she had said. Callison must have had this information on her desk to finally discuss the controversial project with Sarah.

Hearing the emergency vehicles pull into the parking lot, she hastily closed the folder. She didn't need Mark to know that she was snooping around the office of a dead woman. She trotted out of the building, meeting Mark just as he stepped out of his car. Thompson arrived in another car, followed by four deputies and an ambulance.

Browning looked at Sarah, his eyes revealing a mixed bag of emotions. He wanted to enfold her in his arms, protect her from the horror she had just seen. He also wanted to scream at her for putting herself in the danger he had just warned her about. Instead, they stared at each other for a moment, waiting for someone to say something.

"What happened?" Browning breathed, steadying her still-trembling body with hands on both her shoulders.

She leaned against his car, opening her mouth to speak but not knowing where to begin. Browning looked up at Thompson, who was walking toward them, and waved at him to go inside the building with the deputies.

"Take it easy, babe," he said calmly. "Tell me what you saw."

She held her fingers to her temple, squeezing her eyes shut to remember how it all began. "I had an appointment with Beth Callison," she said in a shaky voice. "She told me she wanted to discuss the murder and the building project."

Browning folded his arms and exhaled a loud, annoyed, puff of air. "She should have come to us."

Sarah looked up at him. "She said she was afraid to—that she thought she would be blamed for something. I think she was going to tell me something important, Mark."

He put his hands on his hips and shook his head. "Then *you* should have come to us, Sarah. What were you thinking? I told you that you could be dealing with dangerous people!"

"Mark," she began weakly, knowing her explanation would not satisfy him. "It's my job. I—"

He stopped her with a wave of his hand. "Whatever. I want you to get in my car and stay there until I come out, okay?" Not waiting for her to answer, he went inside the library with the ambulance crew.

She took a few steps after him, then stopped, staring at the building. One deputy was guarding the door, and he definitely wouldn't let her in. But, she told herself, it was her job to *try*—to put up the good fight, get inside and get the story. Instead, she tiredly ran her fingers through her hair and walked back to the car. She'd been rattled by seeing the bloody results of two murders that week. Sniping at the deputy by the door wouldn't add a thing to her story. And, frankly, Sarah didn't want to see the body of Callison one more time.

She slid into the passenger seat of Mark's car, leaned back on the headrest, and closed her eyes. She'd wait until Mark wanted to talk to her.

Thompson was crouched next to the body when Browning reached him. The detective looked up at his boss, his face pale. Even after all his years of viewing dead bodies, this one was tough to look at.

"Our bad guy did a real number on her," he said. "She's got wounds all over. Looks like a knife did it again."

Browning stood over Callison. "Her arms have defensive wounds on them. Unlike Professor Lichner, she put up a fight."

He followed the spatters of blood into the main room, then saw the smudge on the wall. Looking back and forth between the body and the blood stains, he formed a scenario.

"The library closed early today, right? She was probably alone. I'd say the perp confronted her somewhere else in this building, maybe in her office, maybe by the front desk. She saw what was coming and tried to run out the back door, he attacked her, and she just couldn't make it."

Browning grimaced, rubbing his hand over his face. He shook his head as one of the paramedics approached the body. Medical attention wouldn't be necessary, he told her.

Joe Barone and Doc Fellows arrived together, immediately getting to work. Unlike the small classroom where Lichner had been found, the technician had a myriad of surfaces and spaces that he would need to groom for evidence.

"Don't forget her office, Joe," Browning reminded him. "Let's you and I go take a look at it now, Charlie."

They entered it with eyes peeled for any sign of struggle. Objects out of place or blood on the walls could hold valuable clues. But nothing seemed unusual. In fact, Browning noted how tidy the room was. Other than a nameplate, a lamp, and a few office supplies, even her desk held only one simple folder on its surface.

"If the killer came here first, she must have bolted pretty quickly," Thompson observed. "Nothing is knocked over or disturbed."

Browning stepped around the desk to look at the folder. With a gloved hand, he looked inside. Many of the documents looked similar to the ones he had studied in the file from Tom Barrett's office.

"More numbers for us to look at, Charlie. She must have planned to talk to Sarah about the renovation project. Wonder what else was on her mind?" He looked at Thompson, who was staring at the floor.

"Whadya thinking, Charlie?"

Thompson shook his head. "This just don't make sense. I was ready to call Miss Callison our main suspect. Now I'm trying to connect the dots with the people we have left. It just don't make sense . . ."

Barone entered the room with a load of equipment and shooed the men out. Browning grabbed the file off Callison's desk before leaving.

Doc Fellows met them in the hallway. "Multiple stab wounds, death no more than an hour or so ago, looks like the fatal blows were probably in her chest. The ambulance crew is wrapping her up and delivering her to my office. How soon do you need my report?"

Browning smiled. He wished some of his younger deputies had the same energy and dedication to work as this old man. "ASAP, Doc. We need something to work with."

Leaving instructions with the deputies to secure the building once the body and Barone had left, Browning and Thompson headed to their cars.

"I'll meet you at the station, Charlie. I'll be driving Sarah there, and we need to talk to her."

Thompson looked sideways at the sheriff. "I'm not so sure I want to be part of *that* conversation," he joked. "You gotta be really steamed at her this time."

Sarah looked at Browning from inside his car, her frightened eyes unable to hide the shock she still felt from her experience. Feeling mellower than his first encounter with her that night, he got in the car and immediately reached over to squeeze her hand.

One of the perks of being the sheriff's fiancée was being questioned in Browning's office rather than the interrogation room. He and Thompson wanted to know what Callison had told Sarah before her murder.

"You won't be violating that stupid rule you reporters have about protecting a source, right, seeing as how Miss Callison probably won't complain much now?" Thompson asked sarcastically.

Sarah liked Thompson and even appreciated his often biting sense of humor, but she looked at him with a frown. "I'm not sitting here making nasty comments about *your* profession, Detective, so how about laying off mine, okay?"

Thompson merely smiled at her and Browning cleared his throat. "Sarah, you said that Beth Callison had something important to tell you. What do you think it was about?"

"She was kind of vague, but said how upset she was trying to deal with Lichner's murder and the project at the college. I know she wanted to talk about both. I'm just not sure if she wanted to vent, or had something substantial to reveal."

Browning scratched his cheek in thought. "Did she mention any names?"

Sarah thought back to their first conversation, which had ended badly. "The first time I talked to her, she alluded to certain students who couldn't adjust to Lichner's teaching style, but she didn't give a specific name. As far as the building project goes, she only said that the board and Tom Barrett were trying to determine what went wrong financially. In this last conversation, she mentioned no one in particular."

Browning sat back and tapped his fingers together, studying Sarah's face. "You wouldn't be holding back anything from us because you want us to read about it first in the newspaper, would you?"

Sarah wondered whether she should be insulted or not. She decided not, because she'd hidden important information from Browning in the past, just as he had often done with her.

She shook her head, but remembered the file she saw sitting on Callison's desk. "No, but I should stress to you that I think she was planning to focus a lot on the building project, if that helps at all."

She decided that she didn't need to tell them of her plan to look into the project more closely. Why was the controversy weighing so heavily on Callison's mind that she wanted to talk to the newspaper? And why was the file sitting on her desk on the night she was murdered?

Sarah sat in Browning's office as the men took care of other matters involving their latest mystery. She needed to wait for Mark to take her back to her car at the library, and he indicated that he wanted to follow her home.

"Are you guys planning to bring in Matt Baker and Heather Bergen to question them?" she asked Browning when he stopped in his office for some paperwork. Her journalistic juices were beginning to flow again. "And how about Tom Barrett? He might have answers about Lichner's involvement in the renovation project, in case there's a link."

Browning smiled. "We have it under control, but thank you for your advice." He didn't tell her that deputies were already trying to locate all three of them.

Sarah yawned loudly. The nervous energy she'd been operating on had dissipated, and she felt exhausted. She tore the wrapping off a chocolate candy bar that Thompson had purchased for her from a vending machine. Browning appeared at the doorway just as she popped the last bite in her mouth.

"Ready to go?" he asked, rolling up the sleeves on his uniform shirt. He'd yanked off his tie hours ago. "I'd like to get back here soon in case Barone or Doc have good news for us."

He helped her into her jacket and she grabbed her notebook off the desk, full of notes she'd written while waiting for Browning to finish his business. She didn't want to forget anything that had happened.

"I've got a deadline tomorrow night for the next issue," she told him as they walked to his car, "so I'll call you sometime in the afternoon for the latest."

They rode in silence to the library. The front entrance had been cordoned off with yellow police tape, but Browning radioed a dispatcher to send a deputy for a special watch on the building all night.

He pulled into the parking spot next to Sarah's car, and both got out of his.

"Let me just check out your truck before you get in," he told her as he circled it, then opened her door and peered inside. He turned to her and nodded. "Okay, but I'm going to follow you home, just to make sure you're safe. I'll probably have a squad car swing by the cottage every now and then during the night."

She didn't protest as she climbed inside. Browning shut the door and she rolled down the window.

"Hey, do me a favor and leave the investigating up to us, all right?" he pleaded, leaning his arms on the windowsill. "Do you believe me now that this is dangerous?"

"I know it is, Mark. I won't do anything stupid."

He narrowed his eyes. "I don't like that answer. We might disagree on what could be classified as stupid."

She chuckled and cupped his chin in her hand. "I love you for being so concerned about me, but please don't worry so much."

He sighed and shook his head in dismay, then leaned inside the window to kiss her.

A loud shot suddenly pierced the nighttime silence as the passenger side window on Browning's car shattered behind him.

Shoving Sarah down on her seat and shouting "Stay down!" Browning grabbed the portable radio out of his car and called for backup. Checking on Sarah again to make sure she hadn't been hit, he yelled at her to stay in the car. He clipped the radio on his belt and pulled his gun from its holster, cautiously trotting toward the library.

As best as he could determine in the instant it was fired, the shot had come from the east side of the building and angled in their direction. He slowly approached the corner of the library, gun poised in front of him, and peered around it. Seeing no one, he pressed his body against the brick siding and shuffled toward the rear corner of the building, gun still drawn.

His feet began to crunch over shards of glass. Looking up, he saw that the window above him had been broken. He stepped back from the building and studied the window. Could the shooter be inside? He quickly dismissed that possibility because the hole was much too small for someone to crawl inside. He continued down the length of the wall, carefully turning the next corner.

Sarah's face was buried in her car seat as she waited for sounds of Mark outside. As the minutes slowly ticked by, she grew anxious, wondering what he had found. She raised her head just enough to look over her dashboard. It was eerily quiet outside, and she saw nothing. Frightened that something had happened to Mark, she sat up and put her hand on the door handle.

Very afraid, but even more worried that Mark had been hurt, she stepped outside the pickup, quietly shutting the door. Heading toward the sound of the shot, her head spun back and forth, looking for Mark—or their attacker. She turned the corner of the building.

Her search was interrupted when a nearby streetlight was reflected in pieces of glass lying on the grass in front of her. She saw the broken window, then looked back toward the front of the building. The window was just about in the area of the building where Beth Callison's office would be. Had the shooter been trying to get inside?

Suddenly, she heard the sound of someone approaching from around the corner as sirens wailed in the distance. Frightened, she began to run back to Mark's car.

"Freeze! Now!" she heard Mark's deep voice shout.

"Mark!" she called, turning to see where he was.

He stood behind her, holding his gun in front of him with two hands. It was pointed at her. His head dropped to his chest when he saw her face.

"Damn it, Sarah!"

She covered her mouth with her hands and walked toward him, shaking her head slowly as she realized what could have happened. "I'm so sorry . . . I was so worried about you," she said, her voice a strangled whisper. "I couldn't just stay in the car."

He looked at her with a cold stare that brought tears to her eyes. "I can't talk about this right now. Go back to the car. You'll be safe there," he said briskly, adding, "He got away."

Chapter Fourteen

Browning directed arriving deputies to search the neighborhood while Barone and Thompson checked out the broken window. He told them he'd be back after seeing that Sarah arrived home safely.

After looking around the outside and inside of the cottage, he told her a deputy would keep an eye on the place throughout the night.

"Call my cell phone if you need me," he said brusquely, turning to leave.

She put her hand on his arm, stopping him. "Mark, I know you're angry. We need to talk about this. I left the car because I was concerned about *you*."

He looked at the ground. "I think you were concerned about your story, but I don't have time to talk about this right now."

He strode to his car and left. Sarah watched him back

down her long driveway, hugging herself as a cold night breeze kicked up off Lake Michigan.

Browning and Thompson had just finished questioning Matt Baker and Heather Bergen, who both arrived at their respective homes to find deputies waiting to give them a ride to the station.

Matt said he had been with a friend all evening at a local bar. The friend, another local troublemaker known to police, vouched for him. Heather claimed that she had been studying at the college library all night, but was unable to point them to a person who would have recognized her being there.

Browning also talked to Tom Barrett, who had called the sheriff at the request of one of the administrators after hearing rumors of the school board president's death. Barrett had been conducting business on campus all evening and was unaware that they had been looking for him earlier, he told Browning.

"The board knows I've been working with you in regard to Philip's death, so the board secretary asked that I call you to verify the news." He was unable to provide any helpful information, but added that he was still working on compiling the financial figures police had requested.

After the interviews, Thompson followed Browning into the sheriff's office, where they discussed the shooting.

"He had a clear shot at me until I leaned my head into Sarah's window," Browning told him. "That's when the bullet went behind me and hit the squad car. Where did Barone find it?"

Thompson was peeling a banana delivered with the rest of a bag lunch that his wife prepared when he called to tell her that it would be a long night. She knew he would be looking for a midnight snack.

"He dug a .38 caliber out of the back of the front passenger seat. You sure was lucky."

Browning slammed his fist on his desk. "I took too long getting to the rear of the building. By the time I reached the back, I heard a car squealing its tires on the next street over. The shooter must have parked over there and run as soon as he fired the shot."

Thompson's cheek bulged with mashed banana. "Don't be too hard on yourself—you had Sarah to take care of first. Barone will check out the tire marks when it's daylight. Whadya make of the broken window?"

Browning put his hand on the file he'd taken earlier from Callison's office. "I'm guessing he was looking for something—maybe this. He planned to break the window and crawl in, but it either didn't work or I interrupted him."

Thompson pulled a plastic sandwich bag filled with cookies from his lunch. "If it was the killer, why didn't he just take the file with him after killing Callison?" he asked with a furrowed brow. "Want a cookie?"

Browning nodded and took a bite from the Oreo. "Maybe he didn't have time. Maybe Sarah arrived at the library before he had a chance to go back to the office and grab the file." He shook his head. "My God, she gets herself into the worst trouble."

Thompson sat back in his chair, wiping chocolate crumbs off his lips. "She's passionate about her work, boss. I can understand that. We're the same way. And the thing is, I think she might have been looking for you when she got out of the car. Maybe it was stupid, but love makes people do stupid things."

Browning looked at his phone. He still wasn't sure if Thompson was right, but he wanted to hear Sarah's voice—just to make sure she was okay. It rang when he reached for it.

"Mark, it's Doc. You want to hear the preliminary results now, or do you want to wait until morning?"

Browning looked at his watch, amazed that Doc already had information for them. "Now is fine, Doc. Thanks for the quick work. Charlie's in my office, so I'm going to put you on speaker phone."

"I hate those dang things, but go ahead, Mark. Am I on?"

Thompson and Browning grinned at each other. "Yeah, Doc," Thompson shouted. "You're on."

"Well, like I said earlier, time of death was no more than an hour before we got there—maybe less. Fatal blow was a stab wound to the heart, but the poor lady suffered six other stab wounds—two in the back and four more in the chest. And she had extensive defensive wounds on her hands and arms. What kind of a nut . . . anyway, let's see what else I have here . . ."

"How about the weapon, Doc? Can you tell us if it was the same knife that killed Lichner?" Browning asked.

"Hard to say, Mark. The width of the wounds were the same, but the depth was shorter. Now, that would make sense if the killer used the same knife, because the broken knife wouldn't be as long as the original. And remember, the break was angled, so that knife would still have piercing abilities. Both deaths were caused by a single-edged blade."

Doc told him he wouldn't have detailed blood and toxicology results for a few days. "But I know this is the stuff that'll help you out from the get-go, Mark, so I wanted to call you right away."

Browning thanked him and hung up just as Barone stepped into the office.

"Whatcha got, Joe?" Thompson asked.

He shrugged. "Not a heckuva lot that you don't already. I collected a large rock and numerous pieces of glass from Beth Callison's office floor, and a few shards on the ground outside. So, it looks like someone broke the glass with a rock from outside the building. He must have thrown the rock, because unless he had a ladder, the window is just too high to reach."

Thompson snorted. "How the hell did he expect to get in?"

"That ledge outside the window is pretty deep, Charlie," Browning offered. "Maybe he figured on breaking the glass, hoisting himself up and then pulling out the rest of the glass to get in. I'm guessing that I arrived in time to screw up his plan, and that's why he tried to take me out."

Thompson raised an eyebrow. "Maybe he—or she—has been planning to take you out all along. Maybe we're getting too close for comfort."

Browning looked at Barone. "Anything else, Joe?"

"I dusted for fingerprints inside and out, and also on the rock. The rock was clean—he must have worn gloves. The blood smudge on the wall is from Callison, and it's not off her hand. She must have brushed the wall with her body when she was running from the guy. And, I have an enormous collection of hairs and fibers, just like from the classroom at the college."

Browning frowned. "I'm still waiting to hear on the raincoat, Joe."

Barone nodded emphatically. "I know—sorry. It's taking a while because fingerprints are extremely difficult to lift from cloth. The crime lab techs are being really careful on this one, and they told me today that they'll be trying an iodine fume process. Keep your fingers crossed. I'll get back to you as soon as I get the results."

Browning rubbed his eyes and stifled a yawn. "I'm beat, Charlie. Let's go home." He glanced at the file he'd taken from Callison's office. "I want to check this out tomorrow morning. My brain's not working good enough to tackle math right now."

Because Browning's car was damaged, Thompson

offered him a ride home. Instead, he found an older marked squad car in the back of the department's lot that had been put out to pasture, used only in instances when a quick replacement vehicle was needed.

Driving home, he silently blamed himself for letting the shooter slip away. When he was a patrolman in New York, the older guys used to laugh at the way he'd dash into a situation with no concern for his own safety. "You're gonna get yourself killed someday, kid," they'd warn him. But, he always got his man.

Why didn't I act quicker? he asked himself. He had his gun on his belt—all he needed to do was run after the guy. He could have worried about calling for back-up later. It was his job to catch him—and he failed.

He remembered Thompson's words. *You had Sarah to take care of first.* He recalled that his first thoughts when hearing the shot were of her—not of finding the shooter. Those few seconds that he took to make sure she was safe probably meant the difference between catching the killer or not.

Pulling into the parking spot behind his darkened apartment—the lonely place he would soon leave to spend the rest of his life with Sarah—he reflected again on his actions that night and came to a sudden realization.

He would do the same thing again.

Sarah arrived at the office the next morning with puffy eyes and a miserable disposition. She had spent most of the night thinking about what had happened, awakening to her alarm no more than an hour after she'd finally fallen asleep.

Holly looked at Sarah with concern when she dropped her purse on her desk and sunk into her chair. "What's wrong? You look like you've been crying."

Sarah said she hadn't slept much—not wanting to admit that she'd also shed a few tears in frustration over her argument with Mark—and then described the events of the night before.

Holly was shocked. "That must be what Martha wanted to tell me when she came bustling into the newsroom a little while ago. I was on the phone."

Sarah drummed her fingers on her desk, deciding she needed a little advice from her colleague. "I had kind of a . . . disagreement with Mark last night. He told me to stay in my car when he went searching for the guy who shot at him. But, when Mark didn't come back for a while, I got scared and went looking for him."

Holly was confused. "You went looking for Mark or for the shooter?" She wouldn't put it past Sarah to initiate the latter.

"For Mark! I'm not *that* crazy!"

Holly raised an eyebrow. "Okay, tell me the truth. Were you really concerned for Mark's safety, or were you trying to get an up-close view of a news story in progress?"

Sarah cringed at her words. "So, you can believe that I'd do something like that just to get a good story?"

Holly nodded apologetically. "Yeah. Sorry. You've done nutty things like that before."

Sarah leaned back in her chair and bit her lip. "That's the first thing Mark thought. I guess he knows me too well too. The thing is, Holly, the thought of getting the story never crossed my mind. I was frantic when I didn't hear anything outside, and I was picturing Mark lying on the ground hurt . . . or worse. I was afraid he needed me, and I wasn't going to stay in the car."

Holly could tell Sarah was sincere. "That's how you feel when you love someone. But, give Mark a break. I'm betting he's just upset because you could have been hurt. He was only thinking about you too."

Sarah pulled her chair up to her desk and leaned on her elbows, chin in hand. "You know what, Holly? I don't care that it got Mark mad—if this would ever happen again, I'd do the exact same thing."

Sarah wrote a draft of the stories on Beth Callison's murder and the attempt on Browning's life. Her deadline wasn't until that evening, so she decided to wait until later to check with Mark on the latest news. It had been difficult, though, not picking up the phone to call him sooner. He hadn't called her before going to sleep the night before, and she hadn't heard from him all morning. Sarah knew he was still upset, and she hated that.

She was editing a story that Holly had written on an

approaching water rate increase when Mr. Jakes stepped into the newsroom. He sat at Holly's empty desk and swiveled the chair to face Sarah.

"I just heard about Beth Callison's murder," he said, his mouth tight. "Tell me all about it."

Sarah recounted the events and updated him on what she knew of the police investigation. She also described what she planned to report in her upcoming stories.

"Hmm," Jakes started, tapping one of Holly's pencils on the desk. "Not good enough. The entire community is up in arms over these two murders. We need to do something stronger. Write us an editorial."

"Excuse me, Mr. Jakes? We've already got our two editorials written for Sunday's issue—one on the renovation project at the college and one on the proposal to require a leash law for cats . . . remember?"

Jakes frowned. "So, kill the editorial on the cats. Save it for next week. I want something done on the murder investigations. You should have heard everyone at the chamber of commerce meeting this morning. We've had a couple of resorts already lose bookings because of the bad publicity the murders are giving the area. What's going to happen to our businesses if the sheriff's department continues to drag its feet?"

Sarah reminded him that it hadn't even been one week since the first murder. "I think we should give them a little more time to make some progress, sir, before taking them to task on the editorial page."

Jakes blinked rapidly. "Oh, that's what you think, is

it? Could that be because Mark Browning is your fiancé?"

Sarah could feel the heat rising in her cheeks, and she knew they were probably growing red. She hated it when her flushed face revealed how she was feeling inside.

"That has nothing to do with it, Mr. Jakes," she said as calmly as she could. "I've never let that get in the way of our responsibility as a newspaper. I thought you knew that."

He blinked hard again. "You're right—you never have let that sway your opinions, and you're not going to start now. That's why you have to write that editorial."

Her shoulders sagged as she realized he wouldn't back down. It was the publisher's right to request an editorial—after all, he owned the paper. All Sarah could hope for was that he wouldn't demand to read it before it went to print. She planned to write as gentle an admonition of the sheriff's department as possible. Usually, he trusted her judgment.

"Okay, Mr. Jakes. I'll do it right now," she said weakly.

Jakes responded with a hardy nod and stood to leave. "And Sarah, be sure to mention the sheriff by name. Say that he needs to take responsibility for the lack of progress. Ask why they haven't been more forthcoming with information. Is it because they don't know what they're doing?"

Sarah stared at Jakes apprehensively, waiting for him

to add, ". . . and let me read it before it goes to press."
He didn't.

She held her breath until he was out of the room,
exhaling a loud sigh. Closing her eyes and burying her
face in her heads, she wondered just how mad Mark
would become at this latest turn of events.

Browning was staring at the numbers in front of him,
puzzled. They just weren't adding up.

He had formed two piles on his desk—one with the
bids that the school board had approved for the renovation project, and one with the contractors' final bills
once the work they bid on had been completed. He had
found a complete inventory of final bills in the file he'd
removed from Callison's office. It was enough information to begin checking on while he waited for Barrett
to provide some more.

The school board budgeted $2.5 million for the ren-
ovation project, according to the information Barrett
had supplied earlier. He had also given Browning a list
of the winning bids on all the work involved. Those
bids, from eleven different companies working on the
project, added up to just a few thousand dollars under
the budgeted amount.

This *was* an expensive project, Browning thought
when he added up the bids on his calculator. Then, he
began to total the final bills—the invoices those eleven
companies provided to the college once they had finished their jobs. Browning expected the final total to

nearly match what the original bids amounted to, give or take a few dollars. This was always the case in a government-funded project.

But that's not what his calculator was showing. The final bills came in close to $2 million, more than $500,000 less than the budgeted amount.

"Charlie, come in here, wouldja?" he shouted when he saw Thompson pass in the hallway.

He explained to his detective that he'd found a discrepancy in the financial information between Barrett's and Callison's files.

"I know neither one of us is a math whiz, Charlie, but do me a favor and add these up. I've done it three times, and I keep getting the same answers."

Thompson moaned and grabbed the calculator, grumbling how even his wife doesn't trust him to do the bills at home. After punching in the numbers two times, he came up with the same figures as Browning.

"Could be we're missing some of the final bills."

Browning shook his head. "No way. The bills match the bids exactly—same companies, same work descriptions—everything except the costs. The bids say the work will cost one amount, the bills say they cost less. Somehow, the school board approved an extra five-hundred thousand dollars expenditure that never reached the companies who did the work."

Thompson cracked his gum. "Maybe the work came in way under budget. Maybe the school kept that money in its building fund." He thought a second, then asked, "You say about five-hundred thousand dollars is missing in the bills?"

Browning looked at him. "I know what you're thinking. That's the same amount as Philip Lichner's grant. Guess we have to do some more math, Charlie."

Chapter Fifteen

"We can get a court order to do this, Mr. Barrett, but you'd make it a lot easier on everyone if you grant your permission."

Browning had called Tom Barrett, explaining that he wanted to look at the college's financial accounts held at a local bank. Barrett had balked at the request, insulted that police would think it necessary to delve deeper into financial matters that he managed.

"I told you that I'll have all the necessary records ready for you soon," Barrett stressed. "And I can answer any other questions you might have. Looking into the college's accounts is really not necessary. Why do you want to do that?"

Browning was disturbed by Barrett's reluctance to comply. He didn't want to tell him anything more than necessary. "That's really none of your concern. It's police business."

Barrett reacted with outrage. "None of my concern? You infer that our records are somehow mixed up with a murder investigation and you say it's none of my business? You've got to be kidding!"

Browning let him rant before calmly asking who else had the authority to open the records. "Otherwise, we'll simply get that court order. And I'm sure you're aware that, with the college being a tax-supported entity, that will be no problem at all."

"Well, you're out of luck. The school board president, Beth Callison, would have to authorize such an intrusion. Unfortunately, she is no longer with us."

Browning hung up and dialed the administration building. Within a few minutes, he had the name and phone number of Callison's replacement. Soon after that, he had permission to examine the records from the board's acting president, who said he would notify Hillcrest State Bank immediately.

The bank's branch manager stepped outside her office when Browning and Thompson arrived, motioning them to come inside.

"I've pulled up the college's accounts on the computer, and I'm fairly familiar with them," she said. "I hope I can answer your questions. What are you interested in looking at? The information is quite extensive and broken into different categories."

Browning rubbed his jaw. "We need to focus on the

college's accounts concerning the building renovation project—how much money went into them, how much came out—that sort of thing."

She nodded and turned to her computer. "I believe the college set up separate accounts to manage the project. Tom Barrett could probably provide a lot of the information you're seeking. Have you checked with him?"

Thompson glanced at Browning. "Yes," the sheriff said simply. "We've talked to him."

She continued to punch her keyboard, looking for the building accounts and remarking how complicated the financial records were. "Let's see, here's the building account . . . no, wait a minute, that's just for normal operations. I have to find the one dealing with the project." She tapped on the keyboard again, scrolling down each page that popped up.

"All right, here we go," she said confidently. "The college set up two accounts for the renovation work. I have all the deposits and withdrawals listed. Transfers from other accounts were also involved."

Browning was puzzled. "Two accounts? Why two?"

She sat back in her chair, still looking at the screen. "As I understand it, the college withdrew a budgeted amount from the regular building fund and deposited into a new renovation account. Another account was also established for the deposit of special monies, such as those received from grants. I was told that the board wanted to distinguish between the two different sources of funding."

Thompson cleared his throat. "Do you have a record of withdrawals from the accounts?"

She scrolled to another page. "Yes. Here are the withdrawals from the first account. The college paid each company by check."

Browning asked if he could look at her screen and she offered him her chair. He had brought with him the information he'd compiled from Callison's file and compared it to the final bill amounts listed in the account.

"The figures match," he said, squinting at the screen. "Total bills amounted to just under two million, leaving a small balance in this account." He turned to the bank manager. "But the board budgeted two and a half million, and that's what the beginning balance was in this account. Where's the other money? In the second account?"

"Yes. Another account was established for a grant the college received. It was originally deposited into this account, and then the college authorized its transfer into another." She leaned down to point at the screen. "That's the five-hundred-thousand-dollar transfer you see right here. Unfortunately, I don't have the information on the other account in our system."

"Why not?" Thompson asked.

"Because that account is not held at this bank. We have the routing number, but I believe it is for an out-of-state bank."

Browning was staring at the screen, looking at how

the fund balance quickly diminished when the grant was transferred to a different bank.

"Can you get us the name of the bank where the other account is located?" he asked.

"No problem. I'll be right back."

Thompson looked at Browning and whistled through his teeth. "I'm not a numbers man, boss, but this looks like a kind of half-assed way to run a building project. How do you figure having an account in another state? You thinkin' what I'm thinkin'?"

"I'm thinking something stinks, Charlie."

The manager returned with a small slip of paper and handed it to Browning. "Here's your information. We were authorized to make that transfer from our account to First Trust Bank in Milwaukee, Wisconsin. I remember there was something said about it being the bank that the historic preservation grant people worked with. I have no idea why that mattered, but . . ."

Browning tucked the paper in his shirt pocket. "Who from the college set up this account system, ma'am?"

She looked surprised. "Why, Tom Barrett, of course. He's the college's finance officer and was in charge of the project."

The men stood and shook her hand, thanking her for the information. On the drive back to the sheriff's department, Browning removed the piece of paper from his pocket and handed it to Thompson.

"Who's in Wisconsin, Charlie . . . remember?" he said with a knowing smile.

Thompson twisted a toothpick between his teeth. "Uh . . . the Green Bay Packers?"

"Think back to our conversation with Beth Callison about Lichner's sudden wealth. She had an explanation for it, right?"

Thompson narrowed his eyes. "Oh, yeah. She said his father was giving him gifts."

"And where does his father live?"

Thompson turned and grinned at Browning. "In a retirement home . . ."

". . . in Milwaukee, Wisconsin," the sheriff finished.

Browning was on the phone again to the school board's acting president, requesting that a fax be sent to First Trust Bank in Milwaukee authorizing release of information on a certain account to the Potter County Sheriff's Department. The bank's manager had already spoken to Browning and was waiting for the all-clear. He called Browning back when it arrived.

"It's a personal checking account, Sheriff," he told him. "Would you like me to fax you the records on it?"

"I'd like that, sir, but I have a few questions while I have you on the line. Can you tell me whose name the account is in?"

"Yes, hang on minute." Browning could hear the sound of computer keys tapping. "Here it is. It's a joint checking account. The names are Philip and Henry Lichner."

Browning gave a thumbs up to Thompson.

"Oh, yes," the manager said, recognition in his voice. "I'm a bit familiar with this account. Mr. Lichner called us a while back, wanting to add his name to his father's account. Apparently, he received quite a substantial grant for his work—he said it was like the Pulitzer Prize for historians—and he wanted to deposit it at our bank to help out with his father's expenses. I believe the older Mr. Lichner is in a nursing home. Quite a generous son, I would say."

"Mr. Lichner was murdered, sir. Are you aware of that?"

The manager gasped. "No, I didn't know that. But now that you mention it, I heard some of our account managers discussing a case. They said a customer's son had died and someone else was supposed to replace him on the joint account. They were waiting for signatures, I think. One of the account holders is in poor health, as I understand it. Could that be the elder Mr. Lichner?"

Browning didn't answer him. "Sir, could you look at the account for me and tell me the balance?"

"Sure. Okay, the beginning balance was a relatively modest twenty-six thousand until the deposit several months ago of five-hundred thousand. It was a transfer from another bank. The balance right now stands at just over four-hundred-and-ten thousand."

Browning was scribbling notes with Thompson rubbernecking over his shoulder. "How about withdrawals? What kind of amounts are you showing and when were they made?"

"Um . . . well, shortly after the deposit, there was a fifty-thousand-dollar withdrawal. There's been two other sizable amounts withdrawn—one for forty thousand and another for fifteen thousand. Checks were posted for these amounts. The rest of the withdrawals are smaller. I can fax you this information."

Browning gave him the department's fax number. "Can you tell me who the checks were written to and who signed them?"

"I don't have that in front of me, but I can look into it and also fax copies of the original checks. Would that do?"

Browning asked that he send the records as soon as possible. "And one more thing, sir. I need to know where Henry Lichner lives. Can you tell me the address you have on file for him?"

"It's right here on his account. He lives at the Creekside Retirement Home, 436 Wrigley Drive in Milwaukee. Need his phone number?"

He supplied it to an appreciative Browning and promised that the fax would soon be on its way. Browning hung up and explained what he had learned to Thompson.

"Barrett embezzles the funds and Lichner profits? We're missing a link here," he theorized.

"Yeah, and I'm betting that link will lead us to the murderer, Charlie."

He picked up the phone again and dialed Henry Lichner's retirement home. An operator said she would transfer him to Lichner's nurse. When she answered, Browning asked to talk to Lichner.

"May I ask who's calling?" she said.

Browning told her who he was and explained that he needed to talk to Lichner in regard to his son.

"You do know that Philip Lichner was murdered this week?" he asked.

"Yes—such a terrible thing. I'm not sure if Henry understands exactly what happened. And he's unable to speak on the phone."

"Is he . . . not well?"

"Mr. Lichner suffers from Alzheimer's disease. Lately, he was not recognizing Philip as his son when he would come to visit. It is a very sad result of the disease."

"So, I would assume that Philip Lichner managed his father's finances, is that right?" Browning asked.

She confirmed that the staff would always contact the younger Lichner when questions about his father's expenses arose. "He informed us recently that he shared an account with his father so that he could immediately authorize expenditures, if necessary. Sometimes, I would recommend that he purchase various toiletries or other personal items for his father that aren't provided at our facility."

"I see. Do you know who will be managing his bank account now?" Browning asked.

She sighed. "That's a good question. Philip Lichner left no instructions for us in the event of his death, and he was the only family that his father had. My administrator came to me the other day to consult with me on Henry's condition. She said a friend of Philip's from Michigan had called here saying he was aware of the circumstances and wanted to be placed on Henry's bank account. My administrator asked if Henry was able to make this decision on his own."

"What did you tell her?"

"I told her that would be impossible. Even if Henry once knew this man, I'm sure he wouldn't recognize him now. He certainly is incapable of deciding whether this stranger should manage his finances! We've turned all of this over to the facility's attorney for his recommendation."

Browning asked her if she knew the stranger's name.

"No, but . . . just a minute. Our administrator is just walking by and she might remember. Hold on." Browning waited while the nurse explained the phone call to her boss, then she came back on the line.

"She says it's Barrett. B-A-R-R-E-T-T. First name is Thomas. Does that help?"

Browning and Thompson were mapping out their next investigative strategy when Barone knocked on the door, papers in hand and a big smile on his face.

"Tell me you got the results back on the raincoat," Browning pleaded.

Barone was excited. "These guys at the state crime lab are great! Man, if I had the equipment they have down there, I'd be like a kid in a candy store. I feel like a Neanderthal checking for prints with powder when I could use stuff like—"

"What did they find, Joe?" Thompson interrupted with a shout.

He dropped a piece of paper on Browning's desk with a flourish, saying, "Check it out. They managed to lift some prints from the coat. Some belonged to Lichner. Know who else's they found?"

"Who?" Browning blurted impatiently, scanning the paper.

"Tom Barrett's."

"Yes!" roared Thompson, pumping a fist in the air.

Browning smiled, nodding his head enthusiastically. "They got a hit on the prints the college took when they hired him, right?"

"Yeah, prints on the coat and on some paperwork that we collected during our search. The blood on the raincoat belonged to Lichner, and it's important to know that we couldn't find any fingerprints in blood. That tells us that the killer probably wore a glove when he murdered him—otherwise, he would have surely gotten blood on his fingers when he was putting the knife in the coat pocket. He must have taken the gloves off when he returned the coat to the house and started looking at Lichner's personal stuff."

Thompson held out his hand for Barone's other information. "You find any of Barrett's prints at the scene of Callison's murder?"

Barone shook his head. "No. If he was there, he was wearing gloves."

"What else do you have, Joe?" Browning asked. "Have you checked out Lichner's computer yet?"

Barone held up a finger. "That's another thing I wanted to tell you. Yeah, we looked at it and saw that someone had accessed his money program the night Lichner was killed. The exact time someone started browsing was . . . Charlie, give me the info, please." Thompson handed over the bundle of reports. "Let's see . . . here it is. Someone got into his money program at twelve-fifty-two A.M. What's that, about six hours after he was killed? The computer wasn't password protected—anyone could log on."

"How about hairs or fibers, Joe? Anything there that would help us?" Browning asked.

He shrugged. "Not until we can get samples from some of the other people you're interested in. We found hairs from both Lichner and Callison on his coat and in his house. But, they were an item, right? So, that's not unusual. We also have a couple of unidentified hairs from the coat and the house. And, you can imagine how many we collected in the classroom and at the library. Bring me a suspect and I'll tell you if his hair matches our samples."

Browning smiled and looked at Thompson. "Whadya say, Charlie? Should we bring him a suspect?"

Thompson pulled the toothpick out of his mouth and tossed it at the wastebasket, missing his target.

"Yeah, boss. Let's go find one."

Chapter Sixteen

Sarah wrote the editorial Mr. Jakes demanded with a sick feeling in the pit of her stomach. It was difficult to lambast the man she was about to marry, even though she was trying to do it as gently as possible:

Potter County Sheriff Mark Browning has many questions to answer concerning his department's handling of the Philip Lichner and Beth Callison murder investigations. So far, Browning has been unable or unwilling to answer those questions.

She winced when she re-read the opening lead of the editorial. While her statements were correct, she knew that Mark had reasonable excuses for not revealing critical information to the newspaper. Obviously, Mr. Jakes' patience had worn thin once he discovered that the business community was grumbling about the lack of an arrest.

The rest of the editorial publicly asked the same questions that Sarah had been asking Mark privately. Have they developed important information? Are they close to a suspect? Is the community in danger from a lunatic on the loose?

She ended the editorial with a statement that she hoped would smooth Browning's sure-to-be-ruffled feathers:

So far, the county's new sheriff has brought a high standard of professionalism and excellence to all operations of the department. We hope this remains the case in this urgent matter, resulting in the speedy arrest of the killer of two of our finest citizens.

She knew Mr. Jakes would probably accuse her of coddling her fiancé with the last statement, but she could justify it. After all, it was generally acknowledged throughout town that Mark was doing an outstanding job as sheriff. Even Mr. Jakes had told her that once. She wasn't letting their relationship get in the way of her objectivity.

Or was she?

Sarah printed out the editorial and handed it to Holly, asking her to read it and give her opinion. Holly sat back and studied it, reading Sarah's words two times.

She slipped it back onto Sarah's desk. "Trying to get back on Mark's good side at the end, right?" She smiled.

Sarah groaned. "It's that obvious, huh? Should I change it?"

Holly shook her head. "No, really, I was just kidding. Hey, you really chew him out in the rest of the editorial. Any good editor knows that you don't want to alienate your sources or burn your bridges. An editor with absolutely no personal interest in his or her relationship with Mark Browning would end an editorial like that the same way—softening the lecture a little bit so they don't lose a good source forever. Plus, I'm really looking forward to your wedding and don't want you to blow it. Leave it in."

Sarah laughed, a bit more confident in her choice of words but still dreading Mark's reaction to them. She decided that it might be a good idea to warn him, and took her cell phone into the empty lunchroom. They hadn't spoken since their argument the night before—this conversation could be tough, and she didn't want Holly listening.

He answered his phone brusquely, as if he was busy, but his voice softened when he heard Sarah.

"I was going to call you a little while ago," he told her, "but something came up and I didn't get a chance. I'm glad you called. I miss you."

Her eyes welled with tears and she wiped them with a finger. "I miss you too. I'm sorry about last night. I—"

He hushed her. "I know you were worried about me.

I was worried about you too. We'll talk about it more when I see you."

She was silent for a moment, getting her voice under control, then gave a small laugh. "We'll have something else to talk about too. Mr. Jakes told me to write an editorial that's kind of critical of the murder investigation. I was pretty easy on you, though."

He chuckled. "I bet it was tougher on you than it's going to be on me. I've told you before that I don't care what people say as long as I know I'm doing my job."

She hesitated before asking the next question, not ready to push an already sore topic between them. "I'm on deadline tonight. Is there anything more you can tell me about either murder?"

He answered so quickly that she grew suspicious he was hiding something important. "No, nothing to tell you yet. Hey, I have to go. Give me a call when you're off deadline tonight and maybe we can do something, okay? And promise me you won't do anything else I'd disapprove of!"

"Well, I don't know if I can promise that, but I'll talk to you later." She laughed.

She returned to the newsroom and looked at the story drafts she had written on the murders. Looking at her watch, she knew she had plenty of time to dig something else up before deadline. Mark had already shut her out, so she needed to look elsewhere for information. Who could she talk to?

She paged through her notebook, reviewing the items she'd discussed with Heather Bergen, Matt Baker and

Beth Callison. In her interview with Callison, she'd spent time talking about the controversial renovation project at the school. That had also been one of the items that prompted Callison into scheduling the ill-fated meeting with her. Did it somehow tie in to the murders?

Callison had mentioned that Tom Barrett, the school's finance officer, was looking into the problems. He could be the person who might shed some light on what was bothering Callison so much.

"Holly, could you man the newsroom for a while?" It was always a necessity on deadline day to have someone answering the phones. "I'm going to the college to talk to Tom Barrett about the renovation project. For some reason, that topic kept popping up when I was discussing Professor Lichner's murder with Beth Callison."

Holly turned away from her computer. "Okay. Are you sure you don't want me to do it? I've talked to Barrett a few times."

Sarah shook her head. "No, thanks. I'm feeling this might be important to my murder stories. He kind of knows me too. I had to meet with him for a story on the school board elections last year."

Holly reminded her where Barrett's office was at the college, and Sarah grabbed her notebook to leave. Heading out the office door, she figured that Mark wouldn't disapprove of this plan. After all, she thought, what could happen at a meeting with a college finance officer?

* * *

She pulled the pickup into a parking space in front of the administration building. It was just after noon, so she hoped Barrett wouldn't be out to lunch. Maybe she should have called first, she thought, but she hadn't wanted to give him a chance to decline meeting with her. A surprise visit was sometimes best.

She climbed the stairs to the second floor of the building, where Barrett's office was located. There weren't many people roaming the hallway or inside the rooms—she'd guessed correctly that most were on their lunch break.

The door to Barrett's office was closed. She knocked, waited a few minutes, then knocked again. No answer. Turning to look down the hallway, she saw an open office a few doors down.

A bespectacled older woman with a pleasant face looked up when Sarah rapped on the door.

"Can I help you?"

"I'm looking for Tom Barrett, but he's not in his office. Would you know where I could find him?" Sarah asked.

She pointed down the hallway. "I saw him go that-a-way a little while ago, but I don't know where he was going. Sorry I can't help you."

Sarah thanked her and headed back down the stairway in the direction the woman indicated. She was certain that Barrett had probably left to eat lunch, and decided she would return to the school in a few hours.

She got back in her pickup and put the key in the ignition. Looking back up to turn on the engine, she saw Barrett emerge from the front door of the administration building and head toward a car. She pulled her keys out and grabbed her notebook, planning to jump out and catch up to him before he could leave.

But the look on his face stopped her. As he walked quickly to the car, his agitated face looked back and forth as if he was afraid of being watched. Sarah noticed that one hand was hidden under the front of his open sport coat, and she got a quick glance of what appeared to be some kind of small briefcase he was holding beneath it. She watched him as he nervously pointed his keys to activate his automatic car lock opener. He got inside and leaned down, perhaps putting something on the floor of the passenger's side.

Sarah was intrigued. *What's this guy doing?* She decided that it might be worth her time to follow wherever he was planning to go. The least that could happen was she'd catch up to him and ask if he might have a minute to talk, but she wondered what he was hiding in the briefcase. She inserted her key in the ignition and turned it, waiting to follow Barrett's car from a reasonable distance. She didn't want him to know he was being followed—it might aggravate him and then he'd never talk to her.

He pulled out on the highway and began to head south, away from town. Sarah allowed a few cars to merge between them on the two-lane highway. She didn't want him to notice her car.

They were heading toward a road she recognized. It led to one of the smaller Lake Michigan beaches in the area, but one that she and Mark enjoyed visiting because it was so unique. Along with the usually very private beach, the area contained a small creek leading inland from the lake that emptied into a deep pond, home to all sorts of natural beauty.

Sarah wrinkled her brow. *Was Barrett going to the beach?*

After poring over the faxes from the Milwaukee bank, Browning and Thompson decided on their next course of action.

"My guess is that Barrett's mixed up in the murders, Charlie, but we don't know if someone else worked with him on it. I don't want word getting out that we hauled Barrett in here for questioning, and then another possible suspect gets tipped off and skips town quick. Just in case, I'll go get Barrett and I want you to find Matt Baker. We'll bring him in too."

Thompson nodded. "Sounds right to me. But, are you sure you won't need backup with Barrett?"

Browning shook his head. "I'll be casual and just say we want him to come over to check out some financial stuff we've found. He shouldn't balk too much at that."

Thompson looked skeptical. "Yeah, but do one thing for me. I know when you're in plainclothes that you rarely wear your gun. Be sure to carry it, okay?"

Browning smiled and nodded, opening a locked desk drawer and pulling out his gun and holster. "Your concern is heartwarming, Charlie." Thompson just grumbled and walked out the door.

The sheriff slipped on his holster and loaded his 9

mm with ammunition, resting it in its carrier. Although it was warm outside and his dress shirt was comfortable on its own, he put on the windbreaker jacket he'd brought to work with him that morning, to hide his gun. He didn't want people at the college wondering why a guy with a weapon was walking around the halls.

Heading north toward Hillcrest, Browning mulled over in his head the conversation he expected to have with Barrett. He'd probably have another excuse about not having the financial information the police had requested. Browning would tell him that they found some on their own. Would he please come back to the station to take a look at it? If Barrett refused, Browning would have to get tougher.

Browning cracked the window of the marked squad car, deeply inhaling air tinged with the scent of Lake Michigan, just to the west. The road was a bit busier than usual, a sure sign that summer was on its way. As oncoming cars passed him one by one, he noticed a red pickup in the distance. He wondered if it could be Sarah's, but couldn't imagine why she'd be in that area at that time of the day. He squinted as it neared, peering at the driver.

It was Sarah! He waved, but she didn't respond, looking straight ahead at the highway. Turning his eyes to his rearview mirror as she passed, he saw the pickup slow down, its right blinker signaling a turn.

"Huh?" Browning said aloud, wrinkling his brow. "Why is she going to the beach?"

He slipped his phone off his belt and punched in her

cell number. Listening for her answer, all he heard was persistent ringing until a programmed female voice came on the line, telling him, "The customer you are trying to reach is not available." Sarah must have her phone turned off or not with her, he decided.

Continuing on his way to the college, he thought over possible reasons for her turning on that road, which led only to a small beach they'd visited in the past. He knew she was working on a special section honoring Hillcrest's one-hundred-and-fiftieth anniversary. Maybe that area had some significance in the town's past, he surmised.

As he turned into the parking lot of the administration building, his thoughts turned back to the task at hand. He patted his jacket to make sure his gun was in place, and went looking for Tom Barrett.

Sarah saw a sheriff's department squad car heading toward her as she followed Barrett. Remembering that Mark was driving a marked car because of the shooting, she gritted her teeth, hoping it wasn't him. If he saw her, he'd wonder where she was going, probably convincing himself that she was doing something dangerous again. She didn't want him to know that, once again, she was following a lead in the murder story.

She cringed as the squad car passed her, keeping her head locked straight ahead, but turning her eyes so she could see the driver. It was Mark! And up ahead, she saw Barrett make a right turn. She turned on her blinker and looked in her rearview mirror, relieved to see that Mark was continuing on his journey and wasn't turning around to check on her. *He must not have noticed me.*

She concentrated again on Barrett, asking herself why he would be heading to the beach in the middle of a workday. She knew that it was not that unusual to take a lunch break at a beautiful location, but she wondered why he had acted so nervous before getting in the car to go there. She needed to find out.

The road was a straight shot toward the beach area. With the branches of large maple trees forming a curved hood over the street, Sarah felt as if she was entering a tunnel. She followed Barrett from a safe distance, not wanting to disturb the suspicious trip he was making but too curious to turn around. His car was a speck in the distance as he neared the end of the road, probably preparing to park.

She slowed her pickup to a crawl. Knowing that Barrett would hear an approaching car and end whatever he had planned, she decided to pull off and park on the side of the road. She could walk the rest of the way, she told herself, and quietly watch what he was doing. If it turned out that he was simply enjoying a peaceful lunch, she could tell him that she was doing the same, remark on what a coincidence it was that both were there, and then casually ask her questions about the renovation project. It was a perfect plan, she decided.

Hopping out of the pickup and leaving her notebook

inside—Barrett would wonder why she had it if the lunch excuse became necessary—she started the half-mile hike toward the beach.

Browning ended up in the same office Sarah had—asking the woman inside if she knew where Barrett could be found.

Her eyes crinkled when she smiled at him. "My, Tom's a popular guy today. A young lady was here not too long ago also looking for him. I saw him heading for the stairs a while back. He might be at lunch. Can I give him your name when he comes back?"

Browning declined her offer and checked the other floors in the building. No one had any information for him. He was trotting down the concrete front stairs of the building when he heard someone shout, "Sheriff Browning!"

He turned to look. It was Heather Bergen, and she was walking toward him. Dressed in an unusually demure, calf-length blue jean skirt and short-sleeved, mock turtleneck pink sweater, she approached him with an impudent smile on her face. Browning continued to walk to his car, reluctantly stopping at the door.

"Hello, Heather," he said coldly.

She sidled up to him. "Too bad about your car. Maybe if you'd let me help you in the investigation, it wouldn't have happened."

Browning had grown tired of her fascination with him. "Heather, you've already been charged with one crime. I suggest you stop interfering with our investigation before you're charged with another. And trying to make us believe that you know who the murderer is will not work. I don't want you around me, understand?"

He put his key in the door to unlock it.

"You asked me if I knew that you were marrying that editor girlfriend of yours. Well, you know what I think? I think a newspaper editor shouldn't be marrying the county sheriff."

Browning turned, staring at her. "You wrote that note and left it on Sarah's porch, didn't you?"

She simply laughed and slowly stepped backward. "I should have told her the same thing when I saw her here a little while ago. Your marriage is doomed." She turned on her heels and sauntered away.

Browning got in his car and started the engine, absorbing what Heather had just said. Sarah had been at the college earlier, then apparently decided to head to the beach. It didn't make sense.

He grabbed his cell phone again and brought up the newspaper office number. He waited for Holly to answer the phone. He knew she would be there on a deadline day if Sarah wasn't in the office. She answered on the second ring.

"Holly, I'm looking for Sarah and I heard she was at the college earlier. Do you know why she was over there?"

Browning sounded concerned and Holly guessed that he wouldn't be thrilled to know that Sarah was checking out information for her story. But, she quickly concluded, Sarah hadn't said to keep her plans a secret.

"She wanted to find Tom Barrett to talk to him about the renovation project. Want me to leave a message for her?"

"Yeah, could you do that? I tried to reach her on her cell phone, but she didn't answer."

Holly chuckled. "Probably because it's sitting here on her desk. She must have forgotten it. I'll give her the message if she calls in or comes back."

Browning thanked her and hung up, quickly putting the car in gear and racing out of the parking lot. Sarah must have learned where Barrett was—at the beach.

Chapter Seventeen

Sarah's feet crunched on dried brown leaves from the previous autumn. Barrett's car had disappeared at the end of the road. Sarah knew he probably had made the short turn into a small gravel parking lot on the edge of the pond.

The sound of Lake Michigan waves breaking on the beach grew stronger as Sarah neared the shore. She stepped onto the road's asphalt and continued on her way. She didn't want the sound of crackling leaves and twigs to alert Barrett to her presence.

She was closing in on the area where the thick stand of trees had been parted to create the parking area. Slowing her pace, she knew she had to take cover before reaching the open area. If Barrett was there and not already on the beach, she didn't want to alarm him.

She tiptoed into the woods and spotted a huge oak on

the edge of the parking lot. With long, slow strides, she reached it and held on to the tree's thick trunk, peering around the bark.

Barrett's lone car was parked in the lot and he had the passenger's side door open, removing from the floor the bag she had spotted earlier. He shut the door quietly, then slowly turned his head, surveying the entire area. He began walking toward the pond, continuing to look behind him and to the sides, obviously making sure he was alone.

Sarah strained her neck as far as she could around the tree, trying to keep her eyes on him as he walked out of her line of sight. She moved to the other side of the trunk, but the woods blocked her view. She was compelled to see what he was planning to do, so she needed to move from her secure spot.

She had no choice but to move through the woods, closer to the pond. As long as she could stay hidden in the trees, she would be safe. Suspecting that the briefcase could contain financial documents that he was about to destroy, she knew that witnessing the act would be crucial to her story about the renovation project—and maybe the murder.

She wanted to get on her hands and knees and crawl, making herself even more difficult to spot, but the rough terrain in the woods made that impossible. Fallen logs and sharp-edged rocks would slow her progress, and she needed to get to an observation point quickly. He'd already been out of sight for too long.

Stepping gingerly over leaves and branches, she made her way through the woods, seeing she was getting close to the pond. Then she saw Barrett standing at its edge, case in hand and looking at the water.

What is he doing?

She spotted another large tree several feet away on the edge of the clearing. She needed to reach it and establish her hidden vantage point. She took four slow steps toward the tree, then five more quick ones, pressing herself against the tree as branches cracked loudly beneath her feet.

Barrett turned his head sharply in her direction, his face showing alarm. He narrowed his eyes, peering into the woods, trying to find the source of the noise. Sarah squeezed her eyes shut and held her breath, keeping her entire body hidden behind the tree.

Suddenly, a black squirrel ran behind her and into the clearing, hopping and flipping his tail as the animal turned and headed back into the woods.

Barrett stared at it, then turned his head back toward the pond. Sarah exhaled slowly, thanking God for squirrels and cautiously peeking around the edge of the tree. She watched Barrett as he set the briefcase on the muddy side of the pond, unzipping it. Withdrawing an object, he stood and held it in his hand, looking at it intently as he turned it back and forth.

Sarah saw it clearly as the sun glinted off its broken blade. It was a knife.

Barrett lifted his arm high behind him, then brought

it forward quickly and flung the knife into the deep pond. It hit the water with a small splash.

My God, Tom Barrett is the murderer!

Her body quivered in fear as she hugged the tree. She rested her forehead on the bark, trying to decide what to do. Worried that he'd started to walk back to his car and would see her hiding there, she looked around the trunk again.

Barrett was crouching once more, taking something else out of the bag. He stood again, then held the item up to his face to examine it. Sarah gasped.

It was a gun.

She knew she had to get out of there—fast. She began to run, branches and leaves sounding her presence.

"Stop now or I'll shoot!" Barrett screamed at her. She didn't turn to look as she heard his rapid footsteps gaining ground behind her. She continued to veer around tree trunks and hanging branches as she tried to race out of the woods to her pickup.

She didn't see the fallen log in front of her when she tripped and tumbled forward, hitting her head on a near-by boulder. Dazed, she tried to stand again, holding her head and feeling a warm trickle of blood stream down her forehead. She stumbled again, then felt a hand grip her arm and the barrel of a gun press against her back.

Barrett had caught up with her.

"Stand up!" he shouted, lifting her roughly from the ground and swinging her around to face him, the gun now on her chest. "You're that newspaper reporter, aren't you?"

She didn't answer. Her head was spinning and she felt nauseous.

"Answer me!" Barrett demand, shaking her.

"I . . . I'm Sarah Carpenter from the *Times*," she said weakly. "I just wanted to talk to you for a story. I didn't . . . I didn't see anything."

He smirked. "Yeah, right. You're coming with me."

He turned her around again, pressing the gun against her back and shoving her toward the pond as he kept a tight hold on her arm. They reached the edge of the water, and he told her to face him. She turned around.

"You saw me toss that knife in the pond, didn't you?" he hissed, still holding her arm tightly. "You know that I killed Lichner and Callison, don't you?"

She shook her head, the ache making her dizzy. "I don't know what you're talking about."

"Don't give me that. I'm getting rid of you and this gun the same way. You're both going in the pond."

Sarah looked to each side. The area was clear of trees. She could make a break for it. Mark had told her once that if she ever needed to elude an attacker with a gun, to run away fast in a zigzag pattern. Even an accurate shooter would have trouble hitting an erratic target, he had said. But first, she'd try to talk her way out.

"Why don't you just turn yourself in? I'm sure you must have reasons for doing what you did."

He laughed. "Oh, yeah—I do. But I don't think a judge will be too sympathetic when I tell him that Lichner tried to cheat me out of money, do you? And do you think anyone will feel sorry for me that Callison was going to squeal on us?"

Sarah felt woozy. "You stole money?"

"We didn't look at it as stealing—applying for that grant was Lichner's and my idea. Lichner did all the work to get it for the college, and I did all the fancy financing to hide what happened to it. I just altered the bids that came in on the work, making them add up to five-hundred-thousand dollars higher than what the companies actually charged."

"You tricked the school board," Sarah stated dully.

Barrett smiled. "Yeah—they put more money in the renovation account than they actually needed to pay the bills. All the extra money that the board agreed to spend was there for the taking. And the school board never missed the half a million until some people starting complaining that they paid too much for the project!"

Sarah didn't understand. "But, why did you kill Lichner?"

He relaxed his grip on her and stepped back slightly, the story spilling out after keeping it inside for so long.

"I was stupid to put the money in an account that he controlled," he snapped. "We were supposed to split it, but he only gave me fifty thousand. He said he wanted to wait until the controversy died down before giving me the rest. But I knew he was lying. He was planning to take all of it. He claimed he was responsible for getting the grant in the first place."

Sarah was waiting for him to take his hand off her arm. "But why would killing him get you the money?"

He smiled. "His old man's a vegetable. The money is in his account—I know I can get my name on it. Forging a signature is easier than murder. The bank will never know the difference."

Sarah lifted her free arm to touch her forehead, pounding from her fall on the rock. "But Beth Callison—why did you kill her?"

He shrugged. "She found out about it because she started to ask questions after Lichner gave her expensive presents. He thought it was safe to tell her because she wouldn't want bad publicity for the college. But then they split up, and after I killed Lichner, I knew the cops were asking her questions. I knew it was only a matter of time before she told them everything. I had to get rid of her."

Sarah was feeling weaker. She knew that if she wanted to get away, she'd have to do something soon. "Did you try to kill Mark Browning?"

He frowned. "Yeah—I shouldn't have missed when I shot at him. I was trying to get Callison's school board financial documents from her office so the cops wouldn't find them—they might have led Browning to me—and he screwed up my plans. But, I promise, this time I won't miss."

He let go of her arm and stepped back, lifting the gun and pointing it at her head. It was time to make her move.

Browning sped down the highway, passing astonished motorists who probably were cursing him because he didn't have his lights and sirens activated. If Sarah was in a dangerous situation, the sound of police approaching could make it worse. He'd seen people panic, injuring others or themselves, when they knew they were caught.

Finally reaching the road to the beach and making the turn, he saw Sarah's red pickup parked in the distance on the side of the road. He frowned, wondering why she would park there and hoping Barrett hadn't caught her at that spot.

Please, God, let her be okay, he pleaded as he pulled in behind the pickup. He jumped out and ran to her door, yanking it open. She was not inside, injured or worse, but another fear swept over him. Where was she?

He got back in his car and slowly drove down the road, his head swiveling back and forth as he looked into the woods for signs of Sarah. He saw that he was approaching the parking area near the beach and stopped. It was an open area, he remembered, and if she was there with Barrett, he didn't want to be seen. He needed to surprise him—to have the advantage if a confrontation occurred.

He stopped just short of the clearing and shut the car off. Stepping out of it, he left its door open—even the click of a shutting door could alarm Barrett. Crouching next to the car, he slipped out of his jacket and tossed it on the seat. If necessary, he needed to have full, unbound motion in his right arm—his shooting arm. He covered the 9 mm with his hand and stood, heading toward the clearing.

Almost immediately, he spotted Sarah. She was facing him as she stood at the edge of the pond, but she didn't see him. She was looking at Barrett. His back was turned to Browning and his hand was gripping Sarah's arm. His other hand was holding a gun. Browning could see that they were talking, and Barrett's voice would rise and fall, echoing in the serenity of the pond setting.

He needed to get closer without Barrett seeing or hearing him. Taking the same route through the bordering woods that Sarah had taken earlier, he made his way toward them. After taking cover behind a tree, he drew his gun.

He tilted his head to get a look at Barrett. He was still holding Sarah's arm, loudly admitting what he had done. Browning's heart skipped a beat when he saw blood on Sarah's head. She was injured! He knew he had to act quickly before Barrett did something worse.

Browning knew he had a good shot from that distance, but Barrett was just too close to Sarah. With Barrett's hand on Sarah's arm and the gun pressed to her chest, taking aim right then would have been too risky. But waiting longer could be deadly. He stepped out from the tree and raised his gun.

Just then, Barrett released Sarah's arm and stepped back a few feet from her, lifting his weapon. It was time for Browning to make his move.

He gripped the pistol with both hands and targeted Barrett in its sights, shouting, "Barrett! Drop it now!"

*   *   *

Sarah jerked her head toward the sound of Mark's voice, then fearfully looked back at Barrett. An eerie smile spread across his face and he didn't flinch, still aiming the gun at her.

Suddenly, his eyes flickered and he slowly turned, his raised arm moving with him as he focused his gun at Browning. Sarah saw the barrel of the weapon tremble as Barrett took aim at Mark.

"Barrett!" Browning yelled. "Drop it now or I'll shoot!"

Sarah heard Barrett cock the hammer on the gun and she knew what she had to do. Springing off from the muddy bank of the pond, she flung herself full force at Barrett's legs, her head forcefully ramming his hip as she wrapped her arms around his thighs.

He landed on the ground with a thud, his arms splayed in front of him. She scrambled to her feet, frantically looking for Barrett's gun.

"Sarah! Go!" Mark called to her as he started to run toward them.

She ignored his order, her eyes searching the ground for the gun as Barrett rose to his hands and knees. She couldn't let him get it again to take a clear shot at Mark. Spotting the weapon just a few feet from Barrett at the same time as he did, she leaped off her feet, diving for it.

She landed on top of the gun just as Mark reached Barrett and tackled him.

*   *   *

Barrett struggled with Browning on the ground until he felt the barrel of the sheriff's gun on his head and was warned not to move. Pinning Barrett face down in the dirt with a knee in his back, Browning held his arm with one strong hand and gripped his gun in the other.

He looked up at Sarah, her body covered with mud and blood streaming down her face.

"Do me a favor, babe?" Browning asked calmly between gulps of air. "Check out the glove compartment in my car for some handcuffs."

She moved her uncooperative legs as best as she could, trotting shakily to the car. Climbing in the open door, she looked in the compartment and found a pair of silver cuffs. She caught a glimpse of herself in the rearview mirror, shocked at the gash along the side of her forehead. She had felt her head pounding, but didn't know how badly she'd been cut.

She hurried back to Mark, who was listening to Barrett curse both of them. He cuffed him, still keeping him on the ground with his knee, then pulled his portable radio off his belt and called for backup and an ambulance.

"As long as you're not going anywhere right now, Mr. Barrett, let me advise you of your rights," Browning said dryly.

Thompson arrived at the scene quickly with other deputies, congratulating Browning on the capture.

"I had some help, Charlie," he admitted, winking at

Sarah as paramedics tended to her wound. He had convinced her to ride in the ambulance to the hospital.

"I'll have a car pick you up when you're done being treated and bring you back to the station," he promised. "I'll tell you anything you want to know for your story—almost."

Barrett had asked for an attorney to be present when he was questioned, then barely said a word.

"I heard what you told Miss Carpenter, Mr. Barrett," Browning told him. "I was standing right behind that tree, remember? You might as well tell us the whole story again."

The attorney advised Barrett to remain silent, and he obeyed. He'd be locked up at the station until an assistant prosecuting attorney approved the felony murder and attempted murder charges that were sure to be placed against him. The rest of his fate would be decided at a bond hearing, and then possibly a trial.

Sarah arrived at the station about two hours later, her forehead heavily bandaged. She walked into Browning's office and nearly cried when she saw him, so relieved that they both were safe. He stood and held her shoulders, gently kissing her on top of the head.

Thompson, who was sitting in the office, cleared his throat. "I'll leave you guys alone," he said.

Browning wrapped his arms around Sarah after Thompson left. "What am I going to do with you?" he whispered into her hair. "You just won't listen to me, will you?"

She buried her face in his chest, comforted by his

touch. "I guess I'm a hopeless case. Better give up on me."

He laughed and helped her over to a chair. "Hey, you're approaching deadline, aren't you? I'm guessing you want to ask me lots of questions, although you probably know more about what happened than I do at this point. I'm going to call Thompson back in here so we can hear your story, okay?"

She recounted the day's events for the two men, then Browning filled her in on what would happen next to Barrett. She would have to entirely rewrite the front page stories she had waiting to go in the next day's issue.

"By the way," Browning reminded her, "isn't there a certain editorial that you might want to change, now that we've arrested a suspect in the murders?"

She grinned. "I thought you didn't care what the newspaper said about you."

"I lied."

She curled up on a couch in Browning's office as he tied up loose ends. Later, he drove her to the newspaper office and dozed in the lunchroom while she finished her stories—and replaced the editorial. He wanted to drive her home—a deputy would bring her pickup to the cottage later.

They picked up a bag of fast food and gobbled it at her kitchen table. Despite a lingering headache, Sarah was famished. The physical and emotional demands of the day had left her feeling as if she hadn't eaten in days.

Her pickup arrived shortly after midnight and, satisfied that Sarah was feeling better, Browning decided to head home. She stepped out on the porch with him, and he remembered his encounter with Heather Bergen that day, telling Sarah all about it.

"I'm glad it wasn't a disgruntled reader," she said.

"A jealous nut is better?" he laughed.

He stepped back from her, holding her hands.

"Hey, I forgot to thank you for saving my life. When did you learn how to tackle like that?" he asked.

"How about you? You saved my life too!"

He gazed at her, saying softly, "Well, I guess we owe each other then, don't we?"

She nodded and entered his embrace, kissing him with all her might.

Chapter Eighteen

The church was packed. Even people who weren't invited to the wedding came to see their sheriff and their newspaper editor get married. It was the talk of Hillcrest, and it took place on a gloriously sunny and pleasant day.

Following a short rehearsal the night before, Sarah and Mark had laughed and talked long into the evening with family and close friends who returned to the cottage for a potluck meal. They crowded the tiny house and sat on the porch, watching the sunset in the western sky over Lake Michigan. Browning's parents weren't able to arrive from New York until the next morning, just in time for the wedding.

The ceremony was simple and reverent, ending with the respectful, modified church applause that greets newlyweds. The reception was less restrained, as cele-

227

brants kicked up their heels and rejoiced along with Mark and Sarah. Charlie Thompson, feeling encumbered by his stylish new grey suit, threw his jacket on a chair and loosened his tie, asking the bartender for a drink.

Despite fears that chairs would topple on uneven ground and the DJ wouldn't be able to hook up his sound system, the outdoor reception on the front lawn went smoothly. Sarah had chosen to wear a simple wreath of flowers in her hair and satin ballet shoes on her feet, hidden by her long gown, to make their first dance on the lawn easier. She didn't want to trip on a clump of grass in front of one hundred spectators. As Mark took her in his arms, looking tall and handsome in a black suit, her nervousness that everything would be just right melted away.

Mark's parents had arrived a few minutes late for the ceremony, quietly sliding into a back pew of the church. It wasn't until the reception was underway when Mark led them to Sarah, introducing his parents to her for the first time.

"Mark has told us so much about you," his mother said, stiffly offering her hand to Sarah. "I'm so happy we can finally meet you." His father, tall like Mark, nodded to her and smiled.

"I'm happy to meet both of you too," she responded. "I'm sorry it's taken so long."

His father stepped forward. "What a wonderful turnout you had at the church," he commented. "You must be very popular in town."

She shook her head. "Most of those people were there because of your son. He's done an amazing job in an extremely difficult position. The entire county is grateful to him. I'm sure you're very proud of him, aren't you?" she said firmly, looking directly in his father's eyes.

He nodded, faltering slightly. "Why, yes . . . yes, we're very proud of Mark."

Late that night, when all the guests had gone home and Sarah promised her family that she'd call them as soon as she returned from the honeymoon, the two of them collapsed on the couch, still in their finery.

"You were making sure my father said he was proud of me, whether or not he really is, right?" He smiled.

She grinned back at him. "They're not so bad, Mark. I think they have to get to know their son again after being distant for so many years. Maybe they've mellowed, but they just don't know how to make it up to you. Maybe *you* should take the lead."

He put his hand on hers and sighed. "Maybe I will. I want them to get to know you, too—my wonderful wife. Wife! Doesn't that sound great?"

She leaned over and kissed him on his cheek. "Yes! That sounds great!"

He looked at her mischievously. "Hey, there's something we forgot to do."

"What?" she asked, startled, wondering if they'd forgotten to pay the DJ or say thank you to their guests.

"I didn't carry you over the threshold."

She laughed and looked at the front door. "I don't know if you could squeeze through that tiny door with me sideways in your arms!"

He raised an eyebrow. "Betcha I could get you through the bedroom threshold, no problem," he said, lifting her off the ground with his strong arms as she laughed and hugged his neck. "I never have to say good-bye to you at the front door, ever again."

And the next day, the wedding of Sheriff Mark Browning and Editor Sarah Carpenter made front page news.